I LOOKED BACK AT the pond and squinted to be sure I was seeing what I thought I was seeing. The slanting sunlight was just right, so that the animal tracks in the snow were clearly visible. There were lots of footprints.

But the weird thing was that all of those trails came together at a certain place. Those footprints of mice and grouse and deer all led down the slope right toward the pond. They continued right out onto its ice toward the place in the middle where the ice was broken, and there was an open spot of water like a dark, expressionless eye staring up at the gray sky. All those tracks led out onto the pond. Not one track came back again.

THE
DARK
POND

JOSEPH BRUCHAC

THE DARK POND

ILLUSTRATIONS BY

SALLY WERN COMPORT

SCHOLASTIC INC.

New York Toronto London Auckland Sydney
Mexico City New Delhi Hong Kong Buenos Aires

ISBN-13: 978-0-545-03445-6
ISBN-10: 0-545-03445-0

Text copyright © 2004 by Joseph Bruchac.
Illustrations copyright © 2004 by Sally Wern Comport. All rights reserved.
Published by Scholastic Inc., 557 Broadway, New York, NY 10012, by
arrangement with HarperCollins Publishers. SCHOLASTIC and
associated logos are trademarks and/or registered trademarks of
Scholastic Inc. Lexile is a registered trademark of MetaMetrics, Inc.

12 11 10 9 8 7 6 5 4 3 2 1   7 8 9 10 11 12/0

Printed in the U.S.A.   40

First Scholastic printing, October 2007

Typography by Karin Paprocki
Page 35 contains an excerpt from *Beowulf*, translated by Seamus Heaney.
Copyright © 2000 by Seamus Heaney. Used by permission of
W. W. Norton & Company, Inc.

TO ALL MY NEPHEWS:

STAY GENTLE, STAY STRONG

—J.B.

◈ contents ◈

THE DARK POND

IT'S OUT THERE

IT'S OUT THERE. I can't see the dark pond from the window of my dorm room. Its waters are too far back in the woods, four ridges away along the trails that no one else is stupid enough to follow. But all I have to do to see that place in my mind is close my eyes—just as I used to when my mother told me those old Shawnee tales of hidden monsters. I used to think that nothing was as scary as my mother's stories.

It's waiting there. There in the pond. I don't know what it looks like. I try to see it in my imagination, a huge swirling shadow under the murky surface of the hemlock-brown water. Is it like the two-headed snake in my ancestors' stories that the foolish little boy rescued and cared for, the snake that grew into a giant serpent and began eating all the people? Or is it like those long-armed things with hair all over their bodies that used to hide in the springs where people got their drinking water? If anyone looked down into the deep, clear water of those springs they would see something white glittering on the bottom. They would lean closer to try to make out what those piles of white things were. And when they realized they were piles of human bones picked clean of flesh it would be too late. The long arms of those underwater monsters would grab them and pull them under.

Somehow, though—don't ask me how—I know it's not one of them, not a two-headed snake or a hairy long-armed aquatic carnivore. But even though I don't know what it is for sure, even though all I have is a feeling of something big moving under the surface, I know it's just as dangerous as one of those ancient monsters.

I also know that even though it seems that most people don't like me much, even though I don't have any real friends, it likes me. It likes me so much it wants to eat me. I can feel it.

FEELING THINGS

FEELING THINGS. That is one of the gifts I got from my mother, being able to feel things that other people don't. Spooky, isn't it? That is how most other kids see it. And me. Spooky Armie. Ever since I was really little (which was a looong while ago) I've been teased because I was weird. It wasn't just because I looked different, with my thick black hair and my brown skin. It was also because I said things that other kids thought were strange.

In second grade I transferred to a new school. On my first day there I'd made it through the morning by just keeping my head down so I wouldn't be noticed much, but then came recess. I was out on the playground when I felt that something was wrong. It was like I could hear a bunch of little voices calling for help. A group of kids were gathered in a circle at the edge of the soccer field. When I got closer I saw that they were dropping pebbles onto an anthill. I got in between them and the anthill and held up my hands.

"You gotta stop," I said.

"Why?" the biggest kid asked me. He had red hair that stuck straight up. I think his name was Ray, but I'm not entirely sure. I was in three different schools that year, so all the kids who were bullies or made up clever new names for me kind of blend together in my memory.

Anyhow, instead of saying nothing, which would have been the smartest move, I gave him an honest answer.

"You gotta stop 'cause you're hurting them. The

ants are all upset. They're really scared."

"How do you know that?" the red-haired kid said.

"I can feel it," I said.

"Feel this, weirdo."

Then he pushed me. It ended up with me on the ground, crouched over the top of the anthill, while the other kids poked me and tried to pull me off. Finally a teacher came and broke it up. For the rest of the two months I was at that school the other kids called me Armie the Anteater.

Weirdo. Geronimo. Spookie. Tonto. I won't bore you with all the other nicknames I got over a parade of years and a succession of schools. It sort of changed when, as they say, I got my growth. That happened in sixth grade. Except I didn't just get my growth, I got a good part of someone else's, too. I'd always been stronger than I looked, which surprised some of the bullies who tried pushing me around. But now I was also bigger than I felt. Even though I was so much taller than any of the other kids and people stopped trying to push me around, it didn't mean an end to the names they called me. They just called me names when they thought I couldn't hear them. But most of the time I could.

Of course there were times at a new school when some kids would try to buddy up to me—because I was so big. But I'd gotten so used to being the strange little geek the others pushed around that I just stayed inside myself. Like a kid inside a suit of armor built for a giant. Maybe I wanted friends, but I wasn't going to let them know that. Sooner or later they'd look through the visor of that suit of armor, realize how weird I was, and decide they didn't want me as a friend after all.

People didn't even *have* to make up names for me. My real name was strange enough. Armin. Armin Katchatorian. I can thank my father for that name, him and all our Armenian ancestors. I can also thank them for being built like a bull and for being endowed with just about as much stubbornness as your average buffalo. When something upsets me, my first impulse is to lower my head and charge. Smart, eh?

A part of me knows just how dumb that kind of behavior is. That awareness of my own stupidity is also something I got from my mother.

"Armin, I just know you'll outgrow that headstrong nature, when wisdom comes to you."

So she says. She even said it when they sent me off to this school, with its "personalized counseling and healthful outdoor environment." My mother believes that nature is healing. I pretty much agree with her. It is an Indian thing, I guess. Did I mention that my mom is Indian? As if being half Armenian wasn't bad enough.

We are Shawnee, the people of the South Wind. Another reason I just loved being sent to a school on the side of the coldest mountain this side of the North Pole. But I suppose it was appropriate. Of all the Indians in North America, it may be that us Shawnees got shoved around from place to place the most, even more than the Cherokees. All the way from the Yucatan peninsula to Florida to the Ohio Valley and then to Oklahoma, and every point in between.

And if you know anything about Armenian history, you'll realize that Mom and Dad were sort of meant for each other. Just like the Shawnees, there were lots of people who didn't want the Armenians to have a country or a history—or a future.

Like I was saying, the North Mountains School

is so far north that the locals think the Fourth of July is a skiing holiday. It gets so cold that if you light a match, the flame freezes and you have to thaw it out to start a fire. In the winter the birds don't dare sing early in the morning, because if they did their songs would freeze around their little beaks and they would suffocate.

Funny, eh? But I can't take credit. Those are all Devo's remarks. I'm not that good at expressing myself. According to Grayson, self-expression is one of the Top Ten Tasks I need to accomplish. *Express yourself. Don't keep it all bottled up inside you.* Grayson's my counselor here at NMS and is actually a pretty cool guy. Grayson is what we all call him. He says he prefers it.

But I was talking about Devo, how he is always cracking people up with the clever things he says. He's as quick with his mouth as I am with my stubbornness. Devo can make a joke out of anything. He suffers from an overabundance of wit, as Scoops, one of our teachers, put it.

The first time I met Devo was when I bumped into him while we were in the orientation line.

"Watch it, man," he said, pulling his slender foot

out from under my hoof. "Or I shall hit you so hard, your body will have to take a vacation to visit your head."

I looked at this guy. Built like a six-foot-tall pencil with a birdcrest of red hair on top of his dome.

"You want a piece of me, chief?" he said, poking me in the shoulder with his chest. His breastbone was so sharp that I was lucky it didn't cut me. By the tone of his voice and the look on his face, you could see he was a joker. Just playing around. Only an idiot would have taken him seriously and pushed him. Like I did.

Maybe it was because his red hair reminded me of that kid from second grade. Or maybe it was that I was feeling exiled and angry and sorry for myself and pissed at the entire planet. It was only one little shove. I didn't even draw my arm back to do it, but it flattened him.

I like to watch boxing on TV, especially ESPN Classic when they show fights from decades ago. Like this one fight when Muhammad Ali took on the British heavyweight champion.

Ali walks out and just about floors the guy with

the first punch. But that doesn't end it. The guy pops up again. Ali gives him this *You still here?* look. And *pow!* he flattens him a second time. *Ka-boing.* The guy is up almost before he hits the floor. It's like he's made of rubber. He is dancing around Ali, waving his fists like he's the one who just scored a knockdown. *Pow! Ka-boing.* The guy is up again, Ali is just shaking his head. *Pow! Ka-Boing. Pow! Ka-boing.*

Anyhow, that is the way Devo bounced back up to his feet when I first met him and swatted him like a skinny mosquito. Like the British heavyweight champion. But he didn't raise his fists and dance around me. He just squinted his eyes and wiped a little blood from one nostril. Then he looked at me and said "Whah?" like I had just asked him a question in some strange language. Yeah, the language of stupid violent behavior.

I felt ashamed. No one else seemed to have noticed it. Me shoving him, him falling down and popping up like a yo-yo. It happened fast and we were at the end of the line. But I knew it had happened.

"Sorry," I mumbled. "I'm an idiot."

"Oh," he replied, like I had just introduced myself. "Well, I am David Deveraugh the Third. However, if you ever call me that I shall have to kill you. My friends call me Devo."

He held out his long skinny hand and I shook it.

"Armie," I said. Then, surprising myself, I added, "Please don't call me chief."

Devo nodded, looking like a crane when he did it. "Of course," he replied. "Friends for life?"

"Okay," I said, surprising myself even more. But I meant it.

But I have to go back now and explain something, don't I? I just told you how I met my best friend after having said at the start that I don't have any friends. Well, right now that is the way it has to be. I can't have any friends. It's too dangerous for anyone stupid enough to be my friend.

Especially someone as brave as Devo. I wish I was as brave as he is. He has the kind of bravery where he would shove a friend out of the way of a car and get hit himself—making some funny remark while he was doing it so that you would be both laughing and crying when he got killed. There's no way I could let that happen to him. So I haven't told Devo anything about it.

It's out there. I can feel it. And I am not going to wait for it to come for me.

2

THE DARK POND

THE FIRST TIME
I saw the dark
pond was on
one of my walks. It
being a woodsy
school, the teachers encourage you to take walks
on your own. You are supposed to stay on the
trails, of course, not get too far away from the
campus. But they tell everyone that it is part of
the curriculum for students to just take off. Go
out and commune with nature. Get in touch with
the wild part of yourself, so to speak. As if I was
ever out of touch with it.

I guess that Grayson understands a little bit about how it is with me and nature, though. I have to give him credit for that. Part of the deal with this school is that every student gets a counselor, so I didn't expect much. But Grayson surprised me. The first time I walked into his office he hit the nail on the head. He didn't introduce himself, didn't say hello or ask me to sit down. He didn't look up at me wisely over some open folder full of information, compiled from all my former schools, about my antisocial behavior. He just nodded at me and said in this voice that sounded like a truck going over a gravel road, "So, it's easier for you to make friends with animals than with people?"

"I dunno," I said.

I kept my face expressionless, but I was impressed he had picked that up about me. I could feel myself letting down my guard with him. It was only later that I realized he had sort of cheated. That window he was standing next to when I came in looked out over the little stand of birch trees where I'd been sitting to wait for my appointment. He had probably seen me with those three pesky blue jays that had insisted on sitting on my shoulder and eating half of my darn granola bar.

It was right after the anthill incident in second grade when the birds started to come to me. One day I was sitting at the round table behind our house. Dad had made that table from a wooden telephone-cable spool, painting it with polyurethane until the top was smooth as glass. I was trying to make a list of things that were good about myself. I was feeling so down after the way the other kids made fun of me that I needed to do something to make myself feel better. But it was hard to put even one thing on that list. Then I heard the flutter of wings. A robin landed right on the hand that was holding the pencil. It cocked its head and then I swear it nodded at me. It pecked at the sleeve of my favorite shirt. That shirt had been my favorite for so long that it had loose threads, and the robin pulled one loose. With that thread in its beak, it flew up to a cedar by the house.

I put down my pencil and went to sit by the cedar tree. I sat there for a long time, watching the robin as it flew back and forth, bringing twigs and grass and pieces of string as it built a nest. My list was forgotten. I slept that night without even one bad dream.

The next day, when I tried to pick up my list, it happened again. This time it was chickadees. Not one but three of them. They landed on my shoulders and my head. When I stood up they flew in a circle around me. I couldn't stop smiling. I looked down at that piece of paper and wrote three words: *"Birds like me."*

Having told you that story, you might have the wrong idea about me. I am not an eco-freak. I am not a tree hugger. They make me sick. Tree huggers, I mean. Not trees. Trees are okay. But people who go out to worship nature, wilderness with no people in it, they just bug me. For one thing, nature isn't some cute sweet little bunny. It'll swallow you up if you don't watch yourself. It's not that it isn't beautiful or sacred. It is. More than you know. And it's not that I don't get a thrill when a crow flaps down onto my arm or a chickadee lands on my head—though I have to admit it doesn't thrill me when they start pulling out a hair or two for their nests. Orioles are the worst. They weave those hanging nests you see high up at the end of branches. So they like really long hair—like mine. They'll just keep coming back for more unless you get firm with them. You have got to set some limits when birds take you for granted as a safe landing place. I don't mean you shoo them away or anything. You just have to politely say, "Hey, stop that, you got enough." You know what I mean?

Anyhow, you just have to respect the natural world and remember that you're part of it. We're supposed to appreciate the forest, and a lot of times we're supposed to be using the trees for food and shelter and firewood. Of course you thank them for all that. Thanking the trees, that just makes sense. Hugging them is what is sort of dumb. And there's no such thing as wilderness, my mom always says. There's just home. Although you got to remember, like I said before, that just because it's home doesn't mean the natural world is like totally safe. After all, as they say, most accidents happen in the home. Especially when you aren't careful. And that's how I was the first time I saw the pond. I was not careful.

The ice hadn't thawed yet, and so I thought it

would be safe to walk across it. That was before I knew about the springs under the surface that made the ice thin in places you wouldn't expect. Before I knew other things about the pond. It was drawing me in, you see. It was calling me. It knew I was there. It was waiting under the ice.

That day, I was so glad to be outside and not hearing Grayson's gravelly voice drone on about improving my social skills that I didn't catch on to the fact that something was reeling me in.

Armin, you just have to open up more to people. Just take it one little step at a time.

Yeah. Unh-hunh.

Now, though, in the woods, one step after another meant I was that much farther away from anyone who could give me useful life-skill advice and help me add another positive to my balance list.

I was, of course, not anywhere near the marked trails or the school campus. I was maybe two miles into the woods and another mile over on the other side of the cedar swamp on state land. They were always warning the students not to go too far off the marked trails. Every year at least one or two people get lost up here. They eventually find some of them.

As I headed down the slope toward that pond, I didn't make the connection. About people disappearing, I mean. I didn't peep to the fact that I was being lured in. All that stuff about social skills had confused me. I was sure that nobody really wanted to be in my skills group. Well, maybe Devo did. Maybe even Pits, who seems to think I'm not half bad. Although maybe I was fooling myself. It was dangerous to start liking people and assume they would like you back. Why would anyone else want to make me part of their circle? The farther I walked, the more confused I got. Did I really have some friends now? It messed up my thinking. For the time being, I lost my edge. I walked right toward the pond, almost right into it.

Even covered with ice, the pond looked dark and shadowed. It wasn't that big. Only about half the size of the soccer field at the school. But it was way deeper than you might guess and a whole lot older. I know that now, but then I thought it was just one of those shallow boggy ponds scoured out of the rocks by the last glaciation maybe ten thousand years ago. So I made a beeline for it. Happy little frog hopping toward the big black snake. How dumb is that?

The fox must have thought it was plenty dumb. It trotted right out of the small black spruces and hop hornbeam shrubs and sat down in front of me.

3

THE FOX

I T WAS A FEMALE FOX. I could tell by the look in her eyes. Don't ask me how I knew that. I just did. It is one of those things I can't explain, like why animals seem to like me so much and listen to me. (I'm not sure I should include birds in that, since they don't so much show affection for me as they treat me like I am just a useful part of the scenery.) Bad as I am with most other people, I'm that good with animals. Even dogs and cats buddy right up to me. This cop once brought this specially trained police dog to one of my old schools. It got really embarrassing when his big German shepherd that was supposed to obey its master's every wish kept crawling over to my desk on its belly so it could lick my hand.

"Hi," I said to the fox.

She was right in my way, blocking my path. But I didn't feel it would be right to ask her to move aside. Just because this kind of thing happens to me with animals doesn't mean I take it for granted. It is always kind of a thrill for me. It makes my skin tingle and I feel this warmth all over. It's like I've stepped back again into the old times in one of my mom's stories and I only have to walk around the next turn in the path to see an old-time village with bark houses and cooking fires and people dressed in deerskin all smiling and welcoming me back.

The fox looked up at me. It was close enough so I could touch it. Of course I didn't try to. With wild animals, you shouldn't try to touch them first. That's one problem with most people. They see an animal and they just about all do one of three things:

Number one is run from it. Not a good idea.

Not. A big animal like a grizzly bear or a mountain lion or even a mean dog will chase you if you run away. Good way to get mauled, bitten, or even become the main course.

Number two is try to kill it. Unfortunately, people have gotten real good at this over the ages. That is why most animals give human beings a very wide berth. Animals either get wiped out or make themselves scarce when there are too many humans around. Those two-legged people, the animals tell their little ones, don't trust them!

Number three is, to me, the worst of all. "Oh, isn't it sweet? Let me pet it." My dad, who is almost as cued in to Indian ways as my mom is, says that third response can be described by the three Ds: Disrespectful. Dumb. And Dangerous.

So I just squatted down and nonchalantly studied the fox out of the corner of my eye. It isn't really polite to look straight at an animal. When two animals of different species stare straight at each other, that usually means one of them is thinking about dinner while the other one is making rapid plans to avoid being the entree.

She was such a beautiful animal. I'd noticed

other wild foxes around the school, but I'd never seen her before. You get up before dawn like I do every day, you see things most people don't. Looking at this fox head-on, I saw how fat she was. And it seemed to me like she had that sort of knowing look on her face that female animals get when they are going to have babies. If I had been in this very spot back in January, I probably would have seen the tracks on the snow from that mating dance foxes do with each other. From mating time until having her babies is usually about fifty or sixty days for a fox. So she had to have a den somewhere nearby, one she and her old man dug together.

Which brought a question to my mind. Where was her mate? After they mate, foxes stay together to help take care of the pups. Maybe he was hiding nearby, just making himself scarce. But maybe not. I had one of those feelings, the kind of knowing that makes people call me spooky. This mother-to-be was alone. Her old man was gone, not coming back. She was on her own, like me.

The fox whined. She yawned so wide, it looked like her head would split open. Then she ducked her head down to the snow and stuck her nose into it up to her ears. That was when I noticed the black markings on her back. One wide line went right down her spine, while the other crossed over it from one shoulder to the other. I took a real deep breath then. I'd never seen a cross fox before. Back when they used to trap foxes for their pelts, this kind of fox was really rare and valuable. The old Shawnee people, who never would have dreamed about trapping an animal like this, would have said those markings of the four sacred directions meant she was powerful, maybe even some kind of messenger.

"Jeezum," I said. I couldn't help it.

The fox lifted her head out of the snow and shook it. She had a stick in her mouth. She stood up, trotted over, and dropped the stick on my boot. Then she stepped back and sat down again.

Tentatively, I tossed the stick a few feet away, just using my wrist so I wouldn't startle the fox. She jumped up, ran for the stick, grabbed it, and ran in a big circle around me. Fat as she was, she was really moving, spraying snow. Then she dropped the stick. Not at my feet this time, but farther up the slope, away from the pond. Once again, she sat down.

I walked upslope and picked up the stick. I made a motion as if to toss it downhill toward the pond, but something in the fox's eyes stopped me. I threw it upslope. Just like a terrier, she grabbed the stick, played with it, and dropped it. Farther away from the pond.

I bent to pick up the stick a third time. I had walked away from the pond now. I no longer felt the urge to walk out on its thin ice. Why had I wanted to walk across it? That was the kind of dumb thing I'd usually never do. I tossed the stick a little ways downslope. The fox trotted right down, picked it up, and took it a much longer way back up the hill this time. No playing or running in circles. I swear the fox looked disgusted.

This way, stupid.

As I trudged up the slope toward where the fox was waiting with her stick, it came to me. I got it. I looked back at the pond and squinted to be sure I was seeing what I thought I was seeing. The slanting sunlight was just right, so that the animal tracks in the snow were clearly visible. There were lots of footprints. There had been a small storm the night before. It brought what my mom calls tracking snow—not the light blowy fluff that doesn't show a clear track, but snow just wet enough to hold the impression of the feet that pass.

I saw the tracks of grouse, the little snowshoe feathers on their toes. There were rabbit tracks that looked like exclamation points. There were the dotted-line trails of jumping mice and voles. A deer trail that had been followed by more than one animal stretched back and forth across the top of the slope near the cedars.

But the weird thing was that all of those trails came together at a certain place. Those footprints of mice and grouse and deer all led down the slope right toward the pond. They continued right out onto its ice toward the place in the middle where the ice was broken, and there was an open spot of water like a dark, expressionless eye staring up at the gray sky. All those tracks led out onto the pond. Not one track came back again.

A chill ran down my back. I turned to look at the fox. The stick still lay there, but she was gone. All that was left were her tracks, leading away into the woods upslope.

A hundred questions went through my mind.

But I didn't give myself permission to ask them. I remembered one of the old Shawnee lessons my mother taught me about things you can't understand. When Rabbit tries to understand Lynx, Rabbit ends up understanding what it feels like to be dinner. Sometimes all you need to know about something strange is that you need to get away from it.

I followed the fox's trail away from the dark pond.

4

THE DREAM

I SAT AT THE DESK with my head down, my long hair hiding my face. Usually I keep it tied back in a ponytail and sometimes I put it into a braid. But when I want to be left alone, I wear it loose so that it hangs like a curtain over my eyes. Then you can't see my broad face—so flat it looks like I got hit in the face with a shovel, according to Devo.

I couldn't help but laugh at Devo's remark. I

guess it was because it made me think of the story my mom told me when I was a little kid about when Lynx sneaked up on Beaver. Just as Lynx was about to pounce on him, Beaver whomped Lynx right in the face with his tail and then got away, leaving Lynx with a big flat face. Mom used to tell me a lot of stories like that, until she passed her bar exam and got too busy.

I leaned over the notebook on my desk. My right hand held it open while my left hand played with the little silver cross I always wear around my neck. My eyes were closed, but nobody could see that with my long hair blocking my face. Not even Scoops. He was standing up front, waving his arms (last time I looked) and yammering about this old English poem. He was really excited because it had just been translated by some Irish poet he really digs. I usually like what Scoops has to say. The man has a brain and a half, but he never talks down to us. And his enthusiasm is catching. I mean, anybody who can get a bunch of teenagers talking about a sonnet by Shakespeare has to be good.

Today, though, I didn't want to be enthusiastic. I wasn't daydreaming, I just wanted to hide behind my hair. I am the only guy in school who is allowed to have long hair. When I first arrived at North Mountains, I was told that there was a dress code and hair was part of it. No long hair allowed for boys. I hated what I had to do next, because I'm not really into confrontation, like my mom. I really prefer not to be noticed. But I also did not want, no way, to cut my hair.

"S'cuse me, sir," I mumbled to the headmaster. Then I handed him Mom's letter, the same one I always proffer to every principal, headmaster or kommandant whenever I check into a new institution of learning.

"My son," it reads, "is Shawnee. It is part of our tradition that a young man be allowed to grow his hair long. Kiji Maneto, the Great Spirit, is the one who made it so. It is a sacred thing. Regardless of your school policies, you cannot require him to cut his hair."

That letter, plus the usual follow-up phone call to my mom during which she cited the Native American Freedom of Religion Act and reminded the headmaster that she was a practicing lawyer in Washington, D.C., was plenty enough to convince them. They were lucky that they gave in as quickly as they did. I still remember what my mom did at this military school I attended for a while called the Academy. When the hair thing came up, she demanded a private meeting with the Board of Trustees and got it. There was a grim smile on her face when she came out of the door, leaving a dozen supposedly powerful men sitting stunned around their antique mahogany meeting table and looking like they had just gone ten rounds with Mike Tyson.

So it was that the Academy, with its "proud century and a half of discipline and tradition," hadn't been able to force a buzz cut on me. All they could do was require me to keep it tucked up under my cap when I was in public.

Dad, like Mom, is a high-powered lawyer. That is why they are so busy that they don't have much time for me now. So I've been ending up in private schools far away from the snakepit—as Dad calls D.C.—for the last ten years or so. I liked it better when I could be home with them and they could be home with me. But as they have very carefully explained to me, every lawyer willing to work for the interests of Indians and indigenous people around the world is truly needed.

I know that.

It doesn't make me miss them any less.

Anyway, being in class and semi-ignoring a teacher meant things were sort of back to normal for me. I wasn't all creeped out like I had been last night when all I could think of was trying *not* to think about the dark pond. It was like I had stumbled into a Stephen King novel and some nameless awful evil was after me.

I mean last night was bad. Capital B–A–D. I don't know how many times I woke up listening. Just listening. Like I had heard someone, no, some-*thing*, call me. Not by my name, not with words. But in a deeper, scarier way. The way a river calls to the salmon telling them they have to swim upstream now. Swim upstream and die.

As I lay in bed I thought about the tracks of all those animals leading out onto the surface of the frozen pond. My footprints could have been right next to theirs.

I shivered and burrowed in deeper, wrapping the bedclothes tighter around me. I kept wrestling with my blankets and with my thoughts until just before dawn. Then I fell asleep.

Falling asleep was the worst. No sooner did I close my eyes than I opened them and I found myself standing by the dark pond. There was no ice on it. Instead, leaves were on the trees. Spring. But there were no birds singing, no frogs chirrupping. The only sound to be heard was the slurping noise of feet slogging through mud.

My feet. I was at the edge, wading in. The mud was sucking at my feet. Then something cold and clammy started wrapping itself around my legs. But I didn't stop or pull back. I just kept walking in deeper and deeper. I looked around for the fox. It should have warned me. But it wasn't there. I couldn't get away. The hideous dark black water closed over my head.

When I woke up I had a moment of panic. Something really did have me by the legs! I didn't yell, but I fought back. I reached down and grabbed hold with both hands and yanked as hard as I could. There was a loud ripping sound as the sweaty sheets that had gotten tangled around my legs tore in half.

It had taken me half the morning to reach the

point where I felt even halfway calm. I tapped my pencil on my notebook and let out a sigh. How was I going to stop thinking about that dream from last night?

Just listen to Scoops.

Pay attention to what he's saying, the duller the better, let him take your mind in another direction.

He was reading from the book now. I still hadn't caught the name, but it was a capital-C Classic.

"So times were pleasant for the people there . . ." Scoops began.

Okay, I thought, pastoral, peaceful, just what I need.

Then Professor Scoops read the next few lines and the hairs stood up on the back of my neck.

". . . *until finally one, a fiend out of hell,*
began to work his evil in the world.
Grendel was the name of this grim demon
haunting the marches, marauding round the heath
and the desolate fens. . . ."

5

CREEPED OUT

OUR FEET SCRUNCHED through the
snow. For once Devo wasn't yammering
about something. Good thing, too, for I
was in no mood for it.

Fens, I thought. Fens are swamps, sort of. And
the heath, that's the part of the English countryside

away from the villages. That, in fact, is where the word *heathen* comes from—from the people who lived away from the villages and were following the old ways. The heath is where Macbeth meets those three witches.

Of course.

Don't be so surprised. Just because I am as broad as a barn door and twice as thick (thanks, Devo) doesn't mean I am stupid. I also remember things. Pretty much everything, to be honest. My mom says it's the kind of memory most people had before writing was invented. If I think about something that happened, something I saw, I can almost see it happening again. Like the way I remember what just happened in class.

Scoops finished reading the passage about Grendel, the horrible monster who came from the swamps and liked nothing better than to eat people.

Pits raised his hand. Pits is always doing that.

"Professor Scopson," he asked, "where did Grendel live?"

"It appears," Scoops answered, "that our anti-social friend dwelled at the bottom of a deep, dark pond."

Like I really needed to hear that?

"So does this mean he was the inventor of the first aqualung?" Devo asked. Just about everyone laughed, even Scoops.

Everyone except me.

"This ability," Scoops said, "to pass from one world to the next, from the aqueous environment to terra firma, exemplifies Grendel's supernatural endowment. It is a common motif in tales of the uncanny."

Most of the kids in the class tried to write that down. Partially because they admired the way Scoops could fit more jawbreaking words into one simple sentence than anyone else. And partially because they knew that if they parroted his exact words back to him during the next test it'd mean extra marks for them. Scoops likes to know his classes are paying attention.

But I wasn't paying attention. Not anymore. I wasn't taking any notes. I was just putting my head down farther until my wide nose was touching the wooden surface of the desk. Just when I had finally been able to start thinking about something else, the Grendel tale had brought it all back to me.

Let the bell ring and this class be over.

And finally it did.

Devo and I were halfway across the field when something struck me in the middle of my back. It startled me so much that I roared when it hit. It actually took me a second to remember where I was and to realize two simple things. The first was that I'd been struck by a snowball. Just a snowball. The second was that whoever threw it hadn't meant to hit me. No way. Nobody had that big a death wish. He was probably aiming for Devo.

Sure enough, when I turned around to shoot a murderous glare at the snowball-throwing culprit, twenty feet behind us stood Pits. The fingers of his right hand were still splayed out from the act of throwing.

"Oops," he said.

Pathetic, I thought. Even at that range he couldn't hit what he was aiming for. And he's no better at swinging a bat. Even though he's three times as wide as Devo, Pits is half as athletic and twice as timid.

"Want to eat?" Devo asked. Then, before anyone could answer, he added, "Race you!"

As usual he yelled it back over his shoulder after he had gotten a flying head start. The three of us hit the door to the dining hall together.

As I puzzled over the mystery meat that was making a halfhearted last stand between the two halves of a baked potato old enough to vote, Pits looked across the table at us.

"Did that story Scoops was telling us about Grendel creep you guys out like it did me?" he said as he used his fork to shape his potatoes into a miniature mountain with a ski slope runing down its side. I took a mouthful of tie-dyed peas and carrots. "Mumph," I said. It was all the answer he deserved after whacking me with that snowball.

"Well," Pits said, "it freaked me out. Made me feel like somebody or something was walking over my grave."

He flattened the ski slope and split the mountain in half with his spoon.

Devo raised his eyebrows at me. I ignored him.

"Shoot," Pits said. "I know. I'm an idiot. Everything freaks me out. I wish I was like you, Armie. Scared of nothing and nobody. Shoot."

Shoot indeed, I thought.

6

RESEARCH

A WEEK HAD PASSED since I'd first gazed
down at the dark pond. A week since I
had heard that voice that wasn't a voice.
A week since that fox had stepped in front of me.
For seven days I had been trying hard not to think
about what had happened, trying to tell myself I'd
imagined it. As a result, it was all that I could
think about. I was, indeed, creeped out.

But where other, saner people run away from

the things that scare them, can you guess what my brilliant strategy is? Right. Lower my head and charge.

But I wasn't quite that stupid. Even though I knew I had to go back there, I'd take it slow, scope out the situation. It was the weekend again, so I had plenty of time to do that.

One weekend a month, if you hadn't screwed up so badly that you got too many demerits, you were allowed to leave the campus overnight. You could visit family if they were close enough, go off to see friends, take in a concert, or do an overnight camping trip. You just had to be back in time for dinner on Sunday night.

Though I wanted to, I couldn't see my parents this weekend because they were both out of town. Mom was in Los Angeles at a Native American Litigators Conference and Dad was in Phoenix for a board meeting at the Heard Museum. I needed to talk with them, Mom especially, about all of this. But I couldn't do it over the phone. I've never been able to talk about anything serious over the phone. In fact, I find it hard to use more than one syllable at a time in any phone conversation.

Hi. 'Kay. Yup. Fine. No. Yeah. Bye.

That's typical of my half of a phone dialogue. I'm a little better at writing. And, yes, I do have a computer and I know how to send e-mail. Duh. But I couldn't write about this. I tried, but after seeing the words "Hi Mom" appear on my screen, I realized I just couldn't do it this way. Delete.

And I needed to know more. So I decided to do some research.

I gave Grayson my itinerary. I was going to hike the Long Ridge trail and spend the night in the lean-to below Bald Hill. I was a qualified winter camper, so he had no problem with that. Plus, like you might expect from someone working at North Mountain, he was a hiking nut.

"You know, I'm a winter forty-sixer myself," he said. "Just bagged my last mountaintop in January, Mount Marcy. Saved the tallest for the last. Maybe," he added with a smile, "we can do a high peak together sometime."

"Yeah," I said. But not this time.

I put everything I needed into my pack. The winter sleeping bag, the flashlight, the thermos, my fire-making kit, an extra pair of thermal socks, food enough for three days, all the usual things. Last of all, hefting it in my hand before I did so, I hung my hatchet on my belt.

I knew that they'd have one of the local rangers check later to see if I had actually signed in at the trailhead, so that was where I went first. From there it was a five-mile bushwhack across a series of ridges to get to where I was really headed.

So, by midday, I found myself sitting on the hill above the dark pond, which lay so innocently below the cliff. After getting to within a half mile of it, I had begun to circle in.

Not going in a straight line, I'd figured, would keep me from being caught again, make me aware of the fact that I was being called. I also took it slow, my eyes wide open, listening with my ears and my inner senses as well. I saw plenty of animal tracks at first, but the closer I got to the pond, the fewer footprints there were in the snow. I hadn't felt that strange pull. I was almost disappointed.

I kept an eye out for the fox. No sign. Not even a single fox track. But I wasn't too surprised. I'd been lucky in more ways than one to see her that last time. Although everything was still covered deep with snow, the days were longer now. It was mid-March, the time when female foxes go into their dens to give birth. She was probably down in her hole, taking care of her new cubs. I'd passed one place that had looked to be a likely denning spot. It was a sandy ridge less than half a mile from the pond, but I hadn't climbed it. I wanted to give her and her little ones some privacy.

A nuthatch flew down and perched on the rim of my hat. I pulled some sunflower seeds out of my breast pocket and held out my hand. The nuthatch jumped down and started pecking, hitting my palm twice for every time it hit the seeds. Then a chickadee came fluttering in and I had to dig out more seeds and hold out my other hand. Otherwise they would have been squabbling with each other. Birds can be such a pain. Although it did make me feel a little better to have them as company.

Everything was quiet in the valley below. Probably too quiet. But what did I expect? Something out of *Jurassic Park* to smash its head up through the ice and come howling up the slope gnashing foot-long fangs? An active imagination is not always your friend. Maybe I was just being too sensitive.

Maybe I really was just imagining it all. However, the fact remained that I'd learned a few things as I'd grown older.

One was something that the Shawnees have always known. There are lots of things that can kill you. This world really is a dangerous place. To be so afraid that you cannot live your life is dumb. But to be so unaware that you stumble into danger like a rabbit blundering into a snare is even dumber.

So I sat on that hill looking down on the dark pond. If I waited long enough, I thought, I would see something.

I was right.

7

WATCHING

IF YOU CAN SIT still in the forest, you can become invisible. Make your mind calm as well as your body and you become part of the landscape, one with the trees and the hills. That is part of our old Shawnee way. When we had to fight, our enemies usually found it hard to find us if we didn't want to be seen.

The camouflage jacket I was wearing made it easier for me to blend in as I leaned back against the trunk of a big cedar tree whose overhanging branches reached almost down to the ground. There, in the mottled light and shade, even eyes that were only a stone's throw away would find it hard to see me. Only a quick motion on my part or my scent could give me away.

Animals know this way of becoming invisible even better than people. The moose have come back into the mountains around the school. They're even bigger than cows. A moose can be six feet tall at the shoulder and some of them have horns on them the size of the front bumper on a Cadillac. But big as they are, not many people ever see a moose unless it decides to stroll out into the middle of the road.

The place I had chosen to watch from was good in lots of ways. I had a clear view of the whole valley below, not just the pond but even the stone cliff that rose above it. Half a dozen trees clung to that cliff. The biggest of them, right on the top, was a tall old dead pine with jagged and broken branches. I was far enough away that the trees looked small as matchsticks. If anything moved in the snow-covered valley below, it should be easy for me to see it and far enough away for me to move to safety if it looked dangerous. I had made sure that there was a clear path behind me from my place of shelter.

Always make sure you know your escape route. Dad told me that. Living between the Russians and Iranians on one side and the Turks on the other made every surviving Armenian a natural escape artist. Over the centuries Armenians had gotten really good at knowing the best escape routes. My dad's great-grandfather was one of those who escaped the Turks back when they tried to wipe out the whole Armenian nation, about a century ago. They almost succeeded. Every year on April 25 we light a candle and think about the one and a half million other Armenians who didn't escape in 1913.

My hiding place was also well out of the wind. A lot of people don't understand how important that is when you are outside in the winter. While the sun is shining, you may not notice the wind. But as soon as the sun goes behind a cloud, even a little wind can cut through you like a knife. Of course I had on the kind of warm clothing, layers of it, that would keep in my body heat. When you go to a school in the north country that emphasizes the outdoors, you can take it for granted that you'll know how to dress warm, whether you're a Shawnee or a Saudi Arabian.

I drank a little of the hot cocoa in my thermos, stuck it under my coat, and pulled the wool ski mask back over my face so that only my eyes were exposed below the brim of my insulated cap. Then I watched. Without moving.

As the sun moved across the sky it became clearer to me than ever before that there was an invisible line around the pond. Nothing seemed to come very close to it. I saw rabbits, red squirrels, a family of raccoons, several deer—and every one of them detoured around the pond. Even the little shrews steered clear of it. It wasn't like learned behavior. It was as if they could see or smell or hear—or sense—something that warned them away like the yellow tape around a crime scene. It was creepy.

None of those tracks led in, like before. I wondered why none of those animals had been drawn in. Had they wised up to the danger? Or was it just that whatever was there under the dark water wasn't trying to draw anything in right now? Did it go to sleep after it ate, like a big snake? I didn't have an answer. I just kept watching.

The whole surface of the pond was no longer covered with ice as it had been when I first saw it that day with the fox. The southern edge was completely free of ice. Perhaps it was because the air was warmer or because the sun had been shining on the surface. Or it might have been because of springs bubbling up warmer water from far below. I had no way of knowing for sure, but it troubled me. It made me even more certain than I had been before that the fox had saved me— from falling through thin ice at the very least, if not from something worse that I didn't want to think about.

I kept watching. Eventually the deer came by again. There were five of them. A big one, the buck, was in front. They were gradually moving upslope, heading more or less in my direction. In all likelihood they'd find a place to bed down not far from where I was sitting.

I looked back down at the pond. Quiet, too quiet. Something was going to happen. I could feel it. I just didn't know what or when. I watched as the sun moved toward the western edge of the sky. As soon as it reached the tops of the trees, I decided, that would be it. Whether anything had happened or not, I would be out of there.

True, I had prepared as if I was going to be there all night. Whenever I go into the woods, even for a short hike, I always bring with me the few things I need for a survival situation. Warm clothes, something to make fire, and a knife. I had cleared away the snow down to the earth. That was easy to do, for there wasn't much snow under those overhanging cedar boughs, though it was at least two feet deep all around the tree. I had placed down a layer of dry birch bark gathered from trees by the trail as I walked along. Then I had built on top of it a little tipi shape of tinder and twigs and sticks. All I needed was a single match to make a quick fire.

I had also gathered a good-size pile of dry wood, broken into two-foot lengths, and stacked it beside me. There was more than enough to feed a fire through a whole night. If you have ever tried to find dry wood in the forest, late at night in the winter without a flashlight, then you'll understand why I did this almost as a matter of reflex.

But all of that was just in case I was there overnight. Just in case. And that was one "just in case" I had no intention of experiencing. I'd never worried before about being alone in the woods at night. But this time was different. No way was I going to stay here after dark. Even though I felt warm and comfortable, I was leaving before dusk. I stared down into the valley at the pond. The sun edged down a little closer to the treetops, and I blinked my eyes, just once.

When I opened them, there was nothing around me but darkness. A wave of panic washed over me. I had fallen asleep. I didn't know how long I'd slept and I didn't know how late it was, but the moon had not yet risen. I was alone in the darkness.

Then I heard a sound and I knew I was not alone. Something large was moving in the brush right next to me.

8

THE SCREAM

MY HEART WAS POUNDING. I felt as if my
head was going to explode. Then I realized
I was holding my breath. I let it out a little
at a time then breathed in slowly, forcing my heart
to slow down and my ears to listen. I closed my
eyes. Trying to see was just confusing me. I needed
to let my other senses speak to me before I did
anything. When you get frightened in the dark,
the worst thing you can do is act too fast, jump

up, and start running blindly.

Those who hunt in the dark count on that. Have you ever heard the long, eerie call of a horned owl suddenly coming out of the forest night? I love that sound, even when it startles me. But a mouse or a vole hiding in the leaves or a bird trying to sleep on a limb doesn't love that sound. That call, so terrifyingly close, means death to them. It makes them jump or make some other quick motion that the owl can hear. Then, on silent wings, the owl swoops in with its claws spread out. Wham!

So, with my eyes closed, I stayed still and listened. And the next sound that I heard, a soft snort and then the muffled thump of a hoof on the frozen earth, reassured me. Deer. The small herd of deer that I had seen downslope in the twilight had come to bed down around my cedar. It shouldn't have been that big a surprise. The spot I'd chosen— shelter from the wind, low branches to browse— was a natural bedding area for deer.

Even more than foxes, deer stay in one area of the forest. They must have been able to pick up my scent, because now I could smell them. But they knew I meant them no harm.

The way they were moving around, though, showed that they were nervous. Deer don't go on living for long if they lose that nervous edge. I tried not to think about the fact that they might have come up to huddle around me because there was more safety in numbers.

I did think about lighting my fire, then decided not to. I was warm enough. The fire would bother the deer. Aside from dogs—and the occasional wolf who's thinking about taking that same path his canine cousin took a million years ago when he came trotting in out of the darkness—humans seem to be the only big animals drawn in by a fire.

Hester, another of the kids at the school, is from Australia. She told me that once when she and her da were camping in the outback, he told her to look out into the darkness beyond their campfire. Dozens of pairs of golden-green eyes were staring at them.

"Dingos," her father said. "No worries. Just lonely."

I settled back down against the tree. It was so

late now I figured I would just stay the night. The hood of my parka was folded like a pillow behind my neck and I fell asleep again.

Then I heard the scream.

There isn't any way to describe it with words. All I can say is that it ripped through the night like a flint blade slicing through skin. I banged my head back against the tree trunk so hard that I stunned myself for a moment. A bright flash of light sparked in front of my eyes like a shooting star. It stopped me from jumping up, even though every instinct in me told me to run.

The scream came again. Louder and closer. Something thudded into me, knocking me back against the tree. It was breathing hard, trying to shove by me as its feet churned the earth. I covered my face with my arms to keep from being struck by the panicked deer's hooves as it broke free and thrashed through the low branches of the cedar, trying to escape down the hill.

There was still no moon and the night was dark, but I knew the deer could see better than I could. They were scattering, running panicked in every direction away from the old cedar. Breaking branches, tangling themselves up in saplings, falling, getting up again. The voices of all their ancestors were telling them what to do.

Get away! Run, run! Get away!

Some of them were making bleating noises, almost like sheep. They were scared out of their heads. So was I. But I was also remembering the lessons that both my mother and my father had taught me over the years.

Don't run until you know what danger you are running from. And where it is. Wait. Listen.

A desperate cry came out of the night from farther down the slope. It wasn't the same creature that had made those first screams. Then that cry was suddenly choked off.

I listened for the sound of growling, the sound of something breathing hard as it fed. I knew that last cry must have come from the throat of one of the panicked deer when it blundered into whatever awful creature was out there. But all I heard were the sounds of the other deer as their flight took them farther and farther away, until they could no longer be heard. I strained to listen.

I wasn't sure that I really heard it. It might have been nothing more than my imagination filling in my expectations. But I thought I could hear the soft sound of a body being dragged away through deep snow.

9

FIRE

I KEPT LISTENING. Now even that whisper-soft sound was gone. Had I really heard it? I was sure of only two things. The first was that I was not going to go out there and investigate.

The second was that it was time to light my fire. Way past time.

When I was six years old Mom taught me all the old ways to make fire. I made my first bow-drill kit when I was seven. It took me a whole day to make the fire board and the spindle and the hand piece using nothing but a lock-blade knife. I cut my thumb doing it, and I had blisters on my palms when I was through, but I had done it all by myself.

"Stubborn as a little bulldog," my dad said.

But when he shook his head it was in approval. The only time he'd interrupted me was when he checked to make sure the cut on my thumb wasn't too deep and gave me a Band-Aid.

By the time I was nine I was a total expert on fire making. I could do it with a hand drill, a bow drill, a fire plow. I'd learned the more modern ways, too, from flint and steel to a piece of steel wool and a six-volt battery. More than anything, though, I'd learned that being prepared was the most important part of successful fire making. Without dry tinder and a proper base, it didn't matter how many coals you got from your bow drill.

I reached out in the darkness and felt the piece of canvas that I'd taken from my pack to lay over the sticks and tinder hours ago. Having laid the base for my fire, I hadn't wanted the moisture in the air to get at it and make it hard to light should I finally decide I needed it. The deer, in their frantic attempt to escape, had somehow missed it.

I lifted the canvas off. Then I pulled out my butane lighter.

A lighter? After all those years of learning how to make a fire the old way? All I can do is repeat what Dad always says: "If you've got it, use it."

Or as Mom puts it, "Being Indian doesn't mean being dumb."

The dry pine twigs and the larger dead cedar branches turned into red-and-yellow flames with only a quick swirl of whitish-brown smoke. I fed more branches in, piling them carefully so that the heat in the center of the fire would be concentrated. Soon I was in the middle of a comforting circle of light and warmth.

I sat there the rest of the night. It must not have been long until dawn because I still had a good-size pile of wood left when the sun rose and the clouds that had hidden the moon drifted apart like blue hands letting go of the night.

I don't remember much except concentrating on that fire—that fire and the one long pole I had sharpened with my hatchet and then hardened by placing its tip in the fire until it was blackened. I might have been one of my long-ago European or

Indian ancestors, alone with his fire and his spear, waiting out the cold of the night, back against an old tree, hands ready to lift his weapon. I wasn't thinking what or why. I thought only of feeding the fire and being ready.

One other thing I remember about that wait was feeling something warm running down my face. The deer must have grazed me with a hoof. I had a small cut just below my left eye. I moistened the tips of the two long fingers of my right hand with that blood and then drew two parallel lines across my forehead and two more under each eye. I'm not quite sure why. Maybe someone told me once that warriors would do that so that they could see their enemies more clearly. Maybe I read it. Or maybe I just knew it.

When the daylight finally came, I could afford the leisure of thinking about something other than basic survival. I looked down the slope as I stood in the rising sun and saw a drag mark in the snow. It started only a short distance from my shelter.

Still holding my spear, I walked over and crouched down to look closer. There were no foot-prints to be seen. Just the wide furrow in the snow made by the heavy body of a deer. The drag mark led straight downhill. I didn't intend to follow it.

There was so much mist that I couldn't even see the valley, much less the dark pond. Was it a trick of the change in temperature, the result of the warm air that had drifted in with the dawn touching the cold surface of the pond? Or was something hiding itself? I felt as if a cold wind had swept over me. After putting out my fire, I took the trail that led back to the safety of modern buildings and electric lights, dorm rooms and telephones.

10

HANDOUTS

THE NEXT DAY was a normal one. It had to
be. If it was normal, a day like always, I
could keep myself from thinking about
what had happened the night before. I wasn't about
to discuss it with anyone. They'd either think I was
even more of a whack job than usual or, if it was
someone crazy like Devo, offer to help me.

Could I call my parents? There was no way I
could talk about something this strange over the

phone. Even if I skipped out and took the bus to D.C., by the time I got there I probably wouldn't feel the way I did now. I'd doubt that any of it had even happened outside my own imaginings. Besides, when you are my age, you know there's a world of things you can't talk to your parents about, even great parents like mine. How could I tell them about this indescribable feeling I still had? Even now, when I was doing my best to forget it, I could still feel that pull. It was like a hook stuck in the back of my head. This crazy certainty that I was going to go back to the dark pond. I just had to.

But I couldn't think of it now. This had to be a normal day. A normal day. I ground my teeth so loud as I thought about everything being *normal* that a chickadee turned to cock its head at me in startled amazement.

"Sorry," I said to the chickadee.

I readjusted my backpack and started toward the gym. Maybe I could work out some of my frustration in the weight room. I'd deliberately skipped breakfast to avoid people. As a result, my stomach was growling. My feet thudded against the ground, reverberating in my head like the beat of a drum.

I was a walking sound effect.

I was so tense that I vibrated like a guitar string every time someone spoke to me. Even though I am generally feared and despised, people still— probably out of self-preservation, because they are afraid I'll flatten them if they ignore me—make it a point of greeting me when I walk around the campus.

Fortunately, my usual all-purpose response, a deep-throated grunt, was both what they expected in response and appropriate to the way I was feeling.

"Yo, Armie, whazzup?"

"Garrrrhhhh."

"Hey, Armie."

"Garrrrhhhh."

"Armie, my man."

"Garrrrhhhh."

"Hi, Armie."

"Garrrrhhhh."

"Cool crow."

"Hunh?" Though I didn't stop walking, Hester's words made me turn my head. She'd been looking at my backpack.

"What are you doing there?" I said in a quiet voice.

"Ganh-ganh," answered the crow that had quietly drifted down to perch on my pack.

Even though they are usually looking for a hand-out, whenever a bird lands on me it always makes me feel kind of nice. Even if I know it just eyes me as an easy mark.

The crow turned its head, studying me first with one eye and then the other. It was going to be disappointed. I'd nervously eaten the last box of raisins in my pocket while I was sitting around my fire the night before. I probably burned the box in the fire, but I didn't remember. For all I know I might have eaten it, too. Like I said earlier, I wasn't really thinking. I was in some ancient survival mode where words seem to vanish from your mind.

Anyhow, having missed breakfast, I hadn't yet secretly restocked the front pocket of my camo jacket with the usual half dozen or so boxes of raisins and bags of peanuts I carry around for avian handouts. You have to be careful taking things out of the mess hall like that. The food ladies watch you like hawks. You can get demerits if they catch you stuffing your pockets. Somehow I always manage to elude them.

"Ganh-ganh?" the crow said.

"You going to feed it?" Hester said.

The crow eyed my empty front pocket. I'm surprised he didn't hold a Styrofoam cup with one foot and shake it in front of my nose.

"Ganh-ganh!" More insistent this time.

Someone came up in front of me and shoved a box of raisins in my hand.

"You feed her, Armie. She probably won't accept it from me," Devo said.

I opened the box and spilled a dozen little desiccated grapes out onto my palm. The crow hopped down onto my wrist and began to pick them up, one by one.

"You weren't at breakfast, bro. So I brought you this stuff." Devo held out a handful of fruit. Two apples, a pear, a banana. I shoved them into a side pocket.

Devo smiled down at me. "Oh, no problem at all. I love risking demerits by taking food from the mess hall. I'm not the darling of the mess-hall ladies, like certain people I could name."

Hester giggled. I turned to glare at her, but she just smiled back at me.

"In any eventuality," Devo continued, "Mary, the one whose hair makes it appear that she is wearing a white poodle on her head, pulled me aside and proffered this."

He pulled out a small paper sack stuffed with bags of peanuts and raisin boxes and placed it in my hand.

"'Armin isn't in today,' she says, 'but we know he'll need these for feeding his birds.' You can stop thanking me, Grateful One. Oh, and I almost forgot these." He produced half a dozen granola bars—my favorite flavors.

This time I didn't even glare as I took them from him. It was one of the rules of our friendship—if you could call it that. Devo liked to do things for people but preferred not to be thanked. Then he could needle you about not showing enough gratitude. Real thanks seemed to make him uncomfortable.

I started off again toward the gym. Seeing he'd gotten all the grift he was going to pry out of me for now, the crow flapped off. Hester followed the crow. Devo walked with me.

"You okay today?" he said.

That wasn't like him. He knew I didn't like being

asked that kind of thing. Clearly I was showing too much of my emotions.

"You want to get flattened?" I asked.

Devo nodded. I'd reassured him. Armie was okay, as mean and despicable as usual.

"I'm fine, too," he said. "Thank you for asking."

We were almost at the door. Devo stopped and looked back toward the bare branches of a maple tree where the crow now sat. There was a little wind blowing and the crow had both its wings spread, letting the breeze rock it back and forth in the high branches. He looked kind of like a wind surfer out on a lake. Hester was standing under the tree, her arms held out as if she was being a crow too. She didn't mind if anyone saw her doing it. At times, I had to admit, she was mad cool.

"Guess what?" Devo said. "I think there's someone else like you around."

The image of another broad ugly Armenian Shawnee on campus was too much for me.

"What the hell do you mean, Devo? Another kid who looks like me?"

Devo laughed. "No, I mean another chap who's chummy with chickadees. I spied him for the first time this morning with the ground crew. He must have just been hired. They were trimming dead branches out of that large birch tree. When he descended from the ladder, he just held out his hand and whistled. A whole flock of sparrows flew in to land upon it. Then he opened his lunch bucket and began feeding them bits of bread while the other chaps just stood around in amazement. An old Indian . . . I mean Native American. Cool, huh?"

I turned my back on Devo and shouldered my way through the doors into the gym. Why is it that everyone always seems to think that every Indian in the world is interested in every other Indian? Like when you meet someone, after figuring out what you are, they right away have to start telling you that THEY have an Indian friend and you have just got to meet him. Like all Indians are magnets automatically attracted to each other. Like I even cared. And, anyhow, why would some old Indian guy be interested in a half-Armenian Shawnee kid?

11

HIDING OUT

YOU KNOW HOW crazy it gets in a boarding school when you are getting close to vacation? Imagine being in a herd of caribou at the start of migration time. Or maybe in one of those holding pens just before they open the gates to let the maddened bulls go rumbling down the streets of some little Spanish town. No matter what you do or say, every conversation, every thought, every impulse keeps coming back to one thing—lemme outta here!

When you leaving? Who you riding with? Where

you going? When does your mother/father/step-parent/guardian/chauffeur get here to pick you up?

To avoid that irritatingly mindless litany I had taken sanctuary in one of the places I knew I wouldn't be bothered the night before the week and a half of spring break. Tomorrow was Thursday. Break Day. Or as Devo called it, Bugout Day. I never have much to say to people, and in these last few hours before vacation break I felt even less talkative than usual. I guess it was because of the phone call from Dad.

He apologized. Of course. They would make it up to me. They couldn't help it. They both had to go to Geneva (in Switzerland, no less!) for this unexpected conference. They knew I understood how important their work was. Some things just couldn't wait. (But, of course, I always could.) I could come home if I wanted. But wouldn't I be happier just staying up there at the school over the break? It was already worked out with the headmaster if that was okay by me. Dad knew how I loved hiking in the mountains. He'd heard from my counselor, Mr. Grayson, that I'd been getting out into the woods. Now I'd have plenty of time for that. We'd have other times together. Quality time. (He actually said that!) They'd see me this summer.

I used up more than my quota of *Unh*s and *Yup*s and *Yeah, sure*s in that conversation. Nothing else I could say. I almost varied my menu of responses by asking "Summer in what year?" at the end. But I didn't. I really did understand. I really was proud of what they were doing. I really knew how unimportant my life was compared to the lives of the people they were trying to help. I also knew, trying not to feel too self-pitying, that they both really loved me.

So when Dad said, "You know how much we love you, don't you son?" I just added one final round of my all-time parent replies. "Yeah, Dad. Yeah. Sure."

And that was it. And now I was here, all by myself, in the one building I knew no other kid would venture into the night before B-Day. The school library.

Even though I seem as well suited to them as a bull in a china shop, I love libraries. Next to being out in the woods, reading is my favorite thing to do. I've been that way ever since I was really little.

Mom says it is because she's always read to me. Dad read some too, but with Mom it was part of every day's routine. She read to me before I could walk. She even read to me before I was born.

It is part of the old Shawnee way, she explained. Talking to the not-yet-born. Both the mother and the father talk to their unborn child all the time. That way the child knows it is loved even before it takes its first breath. It is more ready to come into the world. You never have a long and difficult birth with a child who has been talked to before being born.

Mom should know about that. It took her all of ten minutes from the time she got into the delivery room to the moment when the doctor, with some surprise in her voice, said, "Well, here he is already!" Then the doctor handed my father what he said looked like a big blue log to him.

I weighed almost twelve pounds.

Fast as I was, it wasn't easy. I had shoulders like a lumberjack. Mom was so happy when I came out that she says it made her laugh. "Giving birth to you really had me in stitches," is what she still says. I don't know why she thinks that is so funny.

Dad had taken Lamaze with Mom—coaching her on how and when to breathe. So when I was born, the three of us were right there together. Because Mom's doctor was a woman, Dad was the first man to ever hold me. He told me he loved me and then handed me to my mom.

That is how it used to be before my parents began doing the really important things they do now. We were together. The three of us lived in a little apartment with no yard in a bad neighborhood because that was all they could afford. We didn't have the big house in Arlington like we do now.

I know it is selfish, but I miss those times. In my memory, that "ratty little dump" as Dad calls it, that first apartment where we lived, seems as big as the whole world. That great big house in Arlington with all its neat trees and flowers seems so small when I am in it alone and my parents are gone.

Dad was right. I would be happier staying here at the school.

I suppose I didn't have to. Devo overheard my phone call. He offered to let me spend spring break with him and his mom and stepdad in Boston. (It was their turn for him. Summer would be Telluride with his dad and stepmom.) I declined his offer. Then I went to seek sanctuary in the stacks, knowing that Devo would tell everybody he knew that I was staying here over the break. I knew that, just so they could get on my good side, other kids would start asking me if I wanted to go home with them.

As it was, I barely made it through the library door in time. Sure enough, looking like some preppie rescue party, Devo and Pits and Hester were standing in the middle of the quad engaged in deep discussion as they looked toward my dorm. Luckily I had slipped out the back and circled around.

Here in the library up on the second floor, I thought, I was safe. Then I heard the downstairs door open.

"Why, hello," I heard Mrs. Phelps, the librarian say. "What can I do for you young people?"

I peeked over the railing. It was the rescue party. There was no way the three of *them* would have come in here unless they were looking for me. I didn't wait for them to mention my name or take the chance that Mrs. Phelps might not have seen me as I slipped in. Librarians are second only to eagles as far as observing anything entering their domain. I moved toward the stairs. There was one last place to hide—the special-collections room.

Special collections is a room about the size of a small classroom at the very back of the building on the third floor. The door, which doesn't have a window in it, is kept locked. I hadn't been given the combination, but had learned it by watching Mrs. Phelps's fingers as she opened the door for me one time. I punched in the numbers, turned the handle till it clicked, then went inside. I closed the door very slowly behind me so that it made no noise.

I looked around at the shelves of books and file cabinets filled with the stuff that makes up the North Mountains Adirondack Collection. Everything in the room, from rare and limited-edition books to copies of articles and newspapers, had to do with the north-country region, the history and folklore of these mountains.

I went to the Native American section. Mom always told me that whenever I was confused about something, there were always two places I could look—one was to the earth and the other to the ancestors. Then she would tell me one of the old stories.

Maybe it would be a story about how Buzzard ended up with a bald head, or a tale about a boy who always listened to his elders and learned so much that he was able to help his people. She told me how the earth was brought up from under the waters by the birds and animals and then placed on the back of a great turtle. That is why we call North America the Turtle Continent. She would also tell me more recent stories about our great people of the past. A lot of times she would tell me about Tecumseh.

Tecumseh was one of the greatest warriors of all the people. When he was born in 1768, a huge green comet streaked across the sky. Shawnees call the comet the Panther of the Sky, and Tecumseh's name means something like that in the Shawnee language. He tried to bring all the different tribes together in a great confederacy to save us from the white settlers who wanted to kill all the Indians or drive us all out. He never gave up, and he always tried to find a way to protect the people and our land. He wanted to live in harmony with the white people, and he only fought when there was no other way. He lived for his people, and he died for them.

Thinking about Tecumseh is a great way to put your own little problems in perspective. I never feel so sorry for myself when I remember how he always tried to find a way to help. I thought of that now.

Three weeks had passed without anything happening. Winter had started to loosen its grip on the mountains, but whatever had hold of me hadn't let go. The memory of that awful night was still burned into my mind like the embers of the fire I huddled over till dawn. Whatever it was that was out there under that dark pond wasn't going to leave me alone. I didn't know what to do, but I knew I had to do something. Maybe if I looked in the right place, I could find an answer.

I knew a lot about Shawnee stories, but I didn't know much about the stories from this part of the Turtle Continent. If there was something out there besides my imagination, I'd bet that it would be in the old stories.

Some white people claim that nobody lived in the Adirondacks before the Europeans settled here. I knew that couldn't be true. In fact, I'd already read an article about Indians in the Adirondacks in a copy of *Adirondack Life* magazine that they had on reserve downstairs for the local history class. The Iroquois and Abenaki were here. I needed to find some of their stories and see if they talked about water monsters. Because after what happened that night, I knew that it wasn't something normal in that pond that had killed the deer.

Hours later, surrounded by the books I'd pulled from the shelves, I was feeling overwhelmed. The Iroquois and Abenaki didn't just talk *some* about underwater monsters—they talked too much about them. There were giant beavers and strange creatures all covered with hair that lurked in the springs and pulled in unwary people. There were huge horned serpents that lived in the big lakes and could be either dangerous or friendly, depending on circumstances. There were sucking monsters that pulled people in like the undertow in the ocean, and great fish that swallowed people whole. There was Toad Woman, who lured children into the swamps, then drowned them and stuck their bodies under a rock till they rotted so she could suck the flesh from their bones.

There was too much to choose from. None of them, though, seemed quite right. But one story gave me an idea. It was from a book by an old guy named Don Bowman. He wasn't Indian, but he'd

learned lots of stories from Indian people hereabouts. This one story told about a deep pond that was formed when a falling star struck the earth. Animals became scarce and people began to disappear from around that area. Finally some hunters were walking around the pond when a giant fish jumped right out of the water, grabbed one of them, swallowed the man, and jumped back in. The hunters who survived went and got some dynamite and dropped it into the pond so that the giant fish blew up underwater. Big pieces of flesh came floating up to the top and the giant fish were never seen again.

Hmmm.

But where could I get dynamite?

I looked up at the window. I'd not only forgotten that my friends were looking for me, I'd lost track of time. It was completely dark outside.

12

NIGHT WALK

M RS. PHELPS NODDED at me as I walked past her desk. It made me realize that she probably knew where I was all along. It was half an hour past the usual closing time and no one else was in the building. She'd been waiting for me. I was glad I'd taken the time to put all the books and articles back in their proper places. As soon as I walked through the front door of the library, I heard her lock it behind me.

Before I went down the library steps, I looked

around the campus. I could see a few people moving inside the buildings, shapes passing in front of lighted windows, but I seemed to be the only one outside.

I lifted my head to the sky and took a deep breath of the clear mountain air. It was a cloudless night. The faces of the stars glittered down at me. The Shawnees say those stars are ancient beings, watching the earth below. There was a half moon in the sky, so bright that I cast a shadow on the snow.

I zipped up my coat, even though it was not that cold and I was only going to walk to my dorm. I reached into my pocket, pulled out my gloves, and put them on. I slid my hood over my head and tightened the drawstring.

Then I realized what I was feeling. That pull, like a compass needle being drawn toward the north. The dark pond was calling to me. Maybe it was because my mind had already been turned toward it. For the last six hours I'd been utterly zoned out. I had completely forgotten about time, about going to dinner, about everything else.

I do that sometimes. I get so involved in something that I go into a kind of trance. It's like nothing else exists in the world except what I'm focused on. Devo has seen me like that. *Spooky* is his word for it.

Spooky is how it felt. Here I was, in the middle of the school campus, surrounded by the safe, familiar architecture of buildings and walkways and benches, miles away from the dark pond. But those human-made things were only shadows. A part of me felt as if I could just close my eyes and be right next to that deep, hungry water.

I'd felt that pull before, but only when I was within a hundred yards or so of the pond. This time, though, it was like the force of some giant magnet was reaching across the intervening miles, through the hills and trees. I was nothing more than a pile of iron filings.

This is ridiculous, I thought.

Then I noticed that I wasn't standing in front of the library anymore. I was on the other side of the quad, heading straight for the trail that led through the field and into the woods.

What am I doing? I thought. I was feeling more annoyed than scared.

I reached out my hand, placed it against the big

birch tree in front of me, and looked back over my shoulder. There were my footprints in the snow crossing the field. The lights of the campus were now small in the distance.

I wrapped my hand around the branch. If I just held on to it, I wouldn't be able to go anywhere. I closed my eyes, feeling the way you do in a disturbing dream when you know you are dreaming. You just have to convince yourself to wake up.

I can resist this, I thought.

Then I opened my eyes. The branch was still firmly held in my hand, but it had been broken off the tree. I was at the top of a hill, no glimmer of lights behind me. I was half a mile into the woods. I dropped the branch and wrapped both my arms around a pine tree, pressing my cheek against the round metal trail marker that was tacked onto its trunk. The metal was as cold as ice, and it made my eye ache.

Good, I thought. Maybe pain will wake me up.

The light from the half moon was visible even here under the trees. I've never been taught to be wary of walking in the woods at night. Aside from your imagination, there's usually nothing to be afraid of in the northern forest—except for other people. These days there's nothing more dangerous than other human beings. Long ago, when there were animals that hunted human beings—those giant animals, cave bears, lions and saber-toothed tigers that lived here on Turtle Island ten thousand years ago—we had good reason to worry about what was out there beyond the safe glow of our campfires and the doors of our lodges. Maybe the deep memory of those creatures makes some people still feel afraid, so afraid they have to make up new monsters that live in the night. Then they fill their scary stories and movies with them.

Tonight, though, I knew there was no need to create any new monsters. The ones our old stories remembered were bad enough. They were so bad that long ago our heroes had to fight those monsters and destroy them to make the earth safe for their children's children.

I no longer believed that all those monsters had been destroyed. But I knew that unless I could stop this whacked-out, half-asleep journey through the forest, I would find out all too soon whether or not at least one monster was still on the job and, tonight at least, working overtime.

Strangely enough, I still wasn't really afraid. I didn't feel weak or panicky. Instead, I felt really pissed off. I get that way when anybody—or anything—tries to force me to do something I don't like.

I was still holding on to the pine tree. I hadn't gone any farther on my stroll toward being something's midnight snack. I carefully released my hold, turned around, and faced back down the hill. I took one step, and another.

Then a dark shape loomed up out of the darkness and grabbed me.

13

SABATTIS

THE GRASP WAS hard as iron. Two big hands held my shoulders as a tall man thrust his face toward mine. Even in the moonlight I could see that his shoulder-length hair was jet black. His deep-set eyes glinted just as dark from under heavy eyebrows. His face was dark and looked worn like the wood of an old barn—weathered, but still strong.

"Hunh," he grunted. Then he shoved me back-ward and let me go with his hands—even though his eyes still held mine.

The moonlight was bright enough for me to take in the rest of him. He had on a red-and-black plaid wool jacket with wool pants to match, the kind of clothing lumberjacks and hunters used to wear before fleece and all those new space-age artifi-cial fabrics took over, and he wore heavy calf-high black boots.

Then the moonlight reflected off the long canine tooth of a bear that hung from a silver chain around his neck. I knew who he had to be. He wasn't as old as Devo had made him out to be—probably just in his thirties—but he had to be the other Indian. He was the new grounds-crew guy who'd been feeding the sparrows.

Aside from that initial disgusted "Hunh," he didn't utter a word. He just stared at my face like he was either trying to memorize it or look below the skin and bone. I didn't say anything back.

For one, I was still getting my breath back after the way he materialized out of the dark like some-body beamed in on *Star Trek*. Of course, I knew he had to have just been sitting there by the path waiting. It is hard to see anyone at night in the woods if they stay down and stay still, even when the moonlight is bright. It had been a shock. But it was also a relief to realize it was a person grabbing me and not something else.

I also kept quiet, because I was embarrassed. I mean, what could I say? *Hi, my name is Armie. I'm out at night walking like some hypnotized zombie toward my certain doom. Heh heh heh.*

Finally the man sighed.

"Darn," he said. Then he gave me a hard push. "Go."

I stumbled a few steps down the hill. The hand pushed me again, this time on my right shoulder. "Not that way."

I turned off on the trail that cut to the right. I could feel him close behind me. This way was narrower than the main trail that led toward the campus, but I knew it well enough to move along at a brisk pace. It looped around the school and came out half a mile below at a parking lot used by hikers and cross-country skiers.

Maybe somebody else would have asked why we

were going that way, where we were going, and what the hurry was. I didn't. Even though this Indian guy whose name I didn't know yet had spoken no more than five words, I realized that he knew what he was doing. Plus I knew I'd been in danger until he had suddenly appeared.

As the trail became wider and more level, I felt another soft push on my back. I didn't look back, I just started going faster, trotting now. It is stupid to run headlong through the forest at night, but you can go at a pretty brisk pace if you know how to do it. It is always lighter over the top of a path through the woods at night, like a second trail of light where you can see the ribbon of sky. You sort of feel the trail with your eyes and your feet at the same time, and you glide along.

A thin, harsh cry cut through the night. It was long and ululating and totally weird. Even though it wasn't that close, it startled me. I stumbled, but I caught myself with my hands and kept going without slowing up. I'd heard that cry before, far too close last time.

We came out into the clearing. It was so much brighter outside the forest that it was almost like stepping out into daylight. A single truck was parked there.

"Get in."

I went around to the passenger side and climbed inside. He slammed his door, jammed the key in, cranked it, slid the truck into gear, and we spun out of the lot. I didn't turn back to see if anything came lumbering out of the forest into the clearing. I looked at my hands and then pressed them between my knees. It was time for them to stop trembling.

He slowed down after we drove out onto the main road. We kept going until we came to the place where the road starts in to Heart Lake, right in the middle of the high peaks. We drove half a mile; then he pulled over and stopped. The snow-covered mountains were there ahead of us, their folds and ridges perfectly outlined by the light of the moon, their tops sharp against the deep velvet-blue of the sky behind them. The place where we had stopped was one of my favorite spots. I liked to walk here from the school, to sit and look out at the peaks.

I looked over at the guy, sitting there with both

hands on the wheel. Thus far he had spoken a grand total of seven words to me. I figured I owed him at least that many in return, so I'd better get started.

"Thanks," I said.

He didn't turn his head, but he sighed. "Shoot," he answered, easily matching my own conversational brilliance. Clearly I needed to take up a little more slack in our dialogue.

"My name is Armie," I said, holding out my hand.

For a minute he didn't move. Neither did I, stubborn being my middle name. Finally he shook his head and sighed again, a little deeper this time. Without turning his head to look at me, he held out his own right hand and grasped mine in a soft handshake.

"Sabattis," he said.

14

WORMS

S ABATTIS.

That was all he said, and it seemed as if that was all he was going to say. We sat there in silence, both of us looking at the mountains. As if saying his name said it all.

Well, in a way it did. Among Indian people, giving your name to a person you've just met is a big deal. A name is a powerful thing. Giving someone your name means that you trust them with something precious to you. It may even mean that you are making yourself more vulnerable.

Sabattis. That name meant more to me than I think he knew. It meant more now, in fact, than it would have meant a day ago. I'd just read about someone named Sabattis in the library's special collection. He was an Abenaki Indian, one of the most famous Adirondack guides more than a century ago.

"Mitchell Sabattis, the Adirondack guide?" I said.

Sabattis didn't stir, but his lips moved as he spoke softly. "My grandfather's grandfather. I'm named after him."

I waited, but that was it. I was beginning to understand how frustrated people get when they try to pry more than a handful of words out of me. I was still pumped with adrenaline from our flight through the darkness. I couldn't take the silence anymore.

"I have an Indian name too," I said. "At least there is this Shawnee name my mom calls me by sometimes. I've never told any of the kids at school about it. My mom is Shawnee and my dad is Armenian. The name that she calls me is Quoshtoki. She says that means like cataract or waterfall. But there are also times when she says she probably should have called me Wannisucka instead. That sort of means idiot."

"Right," Sabattis said.

I could feel my ears getting red the way they do when I am angry or embarrassed, I wasn't sure which. Who was I trying to talk with? I mean he was Indian, sure, but he was just a member of the grounds crew. Here I was, a kid with a good education, going to this exclusive outdoor prep school trying to force conversation out of this poor guy who had probably never even read a book. I should be ashamed of myself.

I looked down at the floor. For the first time I noticed the box of books I had wedged my feet in next to. I leaned over, grasped some thick books on top of the stack, and held them up so that I could make out the titles on their spines.

"*Advanced Invertebrate Studies,*" I read. "*Annelid Anatomy.*"

Sabattis reached over, removed the books from my grasp, and put them carefully back into the box.

"Clean off your hands before you pick up a book," he said. "Those babies cost a hundred bucks each."

I stared at him, my mouth open.

He looked back at me. "What?" he said. Then he smiled. "What's the matter, kid, never seen an Indian working on his doctorate in zoology?"

I shook my head.

"Get over it," Sabattis said. Then his face got serious again. "How long you had it?" he said.

I didn't ask what. Somehow I knew he meant the way I had of seeing and hearing things, the way the animals and birds relate to me, the way things come to me at times in dreams.

"I'm not sure," I said. "I guess always. It must come from the Shawnee side. Tecumseh was like that too. He could predict the future and he could make things happen."

Sabattis nodded. "*Mteowlin*—that's how we put it in Abenaki. Means being something like a shaman. First noticed it when I was little myself. Makes you get quiet about things, doesn't it?"

It was my turn to nod. We sat for a while in silence, even though there was so much more I wanted to know. But I didn't have to ask the question. Like he was reading my thoughts, he gave me the answer.

"So what can you do with it? Well, one thing you

don't do is go wandering off into the night. Just because you hear something calling your name, kid, doesn't mean you got to answer."

"You've been hearing it too," I said.

Sabattis grabbed the steering wheel with both hands and looked back at the mountains.

"We have stories about it," he said. "This thing that lives in certain ponds but has power like a *mteowlin*. Some even say it is half human and half whatever else it is. Comes, feeds, then disappears and isn't seen again for a long time." He tapped out a slow beat on the wheel. "Long life cycle, maybe," he said.

"You mean like a seventeen-year locust that spends all that time underground in its larval stage."

Sabattis looked pleased. "Maybe your mom was wrong about that second name. What was it?"

"Wannisucka," I said, feeling my face redden as I said it.

Sabattis smiled, stared out the window for a while, and then let out another sigh.

"Right," he said. "Like a locust, but a very different kind of animal, and one with a lot longer life cycle. A life cycle that doesn't enter into the feeding stage until certain things happen. Maybe the water temperature in the winter has to be just half a degree warmer or the acidity has to be at a certain pH. Any one of a number of variables that occur so infrequently that it might be a hundred or two hundred years before it gets to that point where it wakes up hungry and ready to call for take-out."

I brushed the dirt from the trail off my hands and then touched one finger to the cover of the book on top of the stack. *Freshwater Annelid Anomalies*. "So you think it's like some kind of worm?"

"Something like that."

"A worm that hunts deer and eats people?"

"Kid, what humans don't know about worms, about invertebrates in general, would fill more than one library. Worms are tough."

I thought about what he had said. It made sense. Worms are amazing. I mean, you can cut one in half, and one half grows a new head while the other half grows a new tail. Thinking of that, my idea about dynamite didn't sound so good. What if I did succeed somehow in getting dynamite and getting it to go off underwater so that it blew the thing into pieces? All those pieces might just make more little monsters.

"So what's the deal then?" I asked. "You on some kind of research grant to find this thing? Part of your thesis or whatever?"

Sabattis stopped drumming on the wheel. "Nope," he said. "Nobody knows I'm here. Why you think I got that job on the grounds crew?"

"So what are you going to do, study it all on your own?"

Sabattis turned to look down at me over his nose. "You crazy? I'm here to kill the damn thing."

He reached over to poke me in the chest with two outstretched fingers. "And you, Wannisucka, are not going to get in my way."

15

THE BREAK

N O ONE EVEN seemed to notice that I got back so late to the dorm that night. I shouldn't have been surprised. It's just that way the night before a big bugout. People have either already departed or are mentally on their way. No one pays much attention to anyone else, aside from asking them if they've seen their sunglasses or borrowed their sweater. Everybody's packing and planning, getting together and getting gone.

Even Devo didn't really pay any attention to me, despite the fact that he and the other two meddlers had been so intent on finding me earlier that afternoon. I guess they'd finally accepted that I wanted to be left alone. Just in case, though, I made myself scarce at breakfast. I watched from behind the shelter of one of the big pines near the gate as Devo's parents—the ones who had pretended I'd be welcome at their home—loaded his bags into the back of their SUV. Even though he couldn't have known I was there, Devo waved at the pine tree before he got in. Then they drove off. I should have felt good about outwitting them, but for some reason I felt kind of empty.

By the next evening the place was like a ghost town. I was invited to dinner at the headmaster's and I had to go. The headmaster and his wife are decent people. Even though I mostly just grunted like a badger, they acted like they were charmed by my conversation and so pleased to have me as their guest, along with Abdul from Kuwait, Maryat from Montenegro, and Ami from Ghana. There was always a handful of kids who couldn't get home over the holidays because they came from other countries. They kept a skeleton crew in the dining hall to feed us few pathetic refugees.

By the third day of the break I was climbing the walls. I kept thinking about the stuff Mitch Sabattis and I had talked about that night in his truck. After he'd given me the word that I was to stay out of his way because he knew what he was doing and I didn't, he had let down his guard.

He'd shown me some respect by explaining how he'd happened to come here and what he was going to do. While working on his zoology degree, he remembered all the Native stories about water monsters and started making connections between the work he was doing and the old tales. He decided to do research on local legends, and for the last three years he'd been noting things like cycles of disappearances that tied in to those same places where the stories were told. Until he'd come to this part of the mountains, he hadn't found anything significant. But when he had come here and felt something pulling him into the woods, he had found that pond—the same day I saw those footprints and the fox—and he knew he was in the right place, that he'd discovered something from one of his people's stories. He decided to make it his mission to find out what lived in the pond, and to destroy it. The job on the grounds crew at the school made it possible for him to keep an eye on the pond and try to keep people away from it until he decided what to do. I was the only thing he hadn't counted on.

"My mom always says that our old stories have got a truth in them and that they can be understood on a whole lot of levels," I said.

"Sounds like my grampa," Mitch said.

That had led us to start talking more about our families. He had even told me about his fiancée. Then he turned and smiled at me.

"Got a girlfriend, Quashtoki?"

"No," I said. I wasn't sure I liked the turn our conversation had just taken.

"I only ask because I've got this cousin who is sick of dating guys without a brain. The two of you might hit it off." He paused and looked me over. "Does the way your ears are getting red mean you're interested?"

I didn't answer that, but by the time he dropped me off on campus, he'd told me to call him Mitch. I had come away from it feeling like I'd been with an uncle.

However, he was an uncle who had given me the hard word that I was to mind my own business. Since he really did seem to know what he was talking about, I'd agreed. I'd stay out of the woods for the next couple of days, even—or especially—if I felt it calling me.

His plan now was to keep a close watch on the pond for a day or two—using the monitoring equipment in the back of his truck, which included an infrared camera and a night telescope. He had a high-power rifle, a 30.06 with a ten-power scope, but he said he had a hunch that if this thing was what he thought it was, a rifle wouldn't do much to stop it. It'd just make a few holes in it and make it madder. What he was counting on was not dynamite, but this poison he had mixed up to put into the water. Once he was totally sure of what he was dealing with—when he had hard evidence like a sighting or, even better, a pic-ture—he'd use it. I couldn't quite understand how the poison worked, but it was some kind of organic thing that wouldn't hurt mammals or stay in the environment, like the rotenone that they use to kill the fish in some ponds before they restock them with trout. He made it sound easy. I hoped he was right.

That third night into the break, though, I had a dream. It came in a confusion of images. Silent darkness of a hillslope, sound of feet moving through the muddy snow, a jet-black pond growing closer and closer. Still, dark, silent water—then something erupting out of the water, lifting like a glistening tree trunk topped by a mouth that gaped wide. Then running, stumbling, rising to run again, hands scrabbling against stone. I could hear the heavy breathing of a person struggling as he climbed, and then an ear-shattering scream.

That scream was still ringing in my ears as I sat up in bed.

It had been three nights since I'd been on the hillside myself. Three nights since I had answered that wordless call that drew me there. But I hadn't felt that call at all since then, not even once.

There'd been a complete break. It was as if the creature was no longer trying to lure me in. But if it wasn't calling me, drawing me close enough to be taken, who was it calling?

Mitch.

16

THE CLIFF

I TOOK A QUICK glance at my watch as I threw my clothes on. The night was almost over. It'd be dawn soon. Praying I wouldn't be too late—and not at all sure exactly what I thought I was doing—I jammed a few things into a pack, including a hatchet and a strong flashlight. I slipped my buck knife onto my belt.

When you go to an outdoor school, you'll find that most of the students have lots of things with sharp edges. Also, there's a lot of pack rat in me. I have this one wide shelf in my room that is heavy with stray items I've found here and there and brought home. Coils of wire, pieces of string, old tools that someone dropped, odd bits of wood and metal and plastic. From that shelf I grabbed a forty-foot coil of strong nylon rope. Then, as an afterthought, I snagged the three unused road flares I had found beside the Lake Placid highway after a truck breakdown had been towed away. A shoulder-held rocket launcher would have made me feel a little more secure.

You might think I was developing a plan. Maybe so, but for the moment I was doing a great job of keeping it a secret from myself.

I used the flashlight when I got to the woods. I was in too much of a hurry to try to get there in the dark, even though the first light before dawn was just about to make itself visible over the mountains. With the light I could run full speed along the trails.

I wasn't worried about wearing myself out. Years of playing lacrosse had built the kind of endurance you find in a marathon runner.

In the old days, when Shawnees played stick-and-ball games, a game could last a whole day and the goals might be more than a mile apart. I always played modern lacrosse with the idea of that old Shawnee game in the back of my head. Kind of like the Tarahumara runners from Mexico. Those guys will run a hundred miles just to swing by a friend's house and say "Whazzup?" When the first Tarahumara runners took part in the Olympics, they nonchalantly trotted across the finish line way behind the winners, but they didn't stop. They just kept going. When people caught up to them and told them that the race was over, the Tarahumaras were shocked.

"What?" they said. "We thought this was supposed to be a long race. We didn't know it was that short."

It wasn't a hundred or even twenty-six miles to reach the hilltop where I could see the dark pond, but it seemed that long. Fast as I ran, I felt like I'd never get there. Or that when I got there it would be too late. Way too late.

I'd been seeing footprints in the snow for half a mile by the time I reached the hilltop. The tracks had come in off that branch trail that led to the highway parking spot. I recognized them as most likely Mitch's from the size of the print and the shape of the treads. But aside from the tracks, I saw no sign of anyone. I heard nothing more than the huffing of my own breath and the muffled thudding of my own running feet.

The sky was glowing now. Dawn comes later in the mountains, but the light reaches you before the first sight of the sun itself. By now the birds should have been starting to stir. But there was no sign of them. No chickadees or nuthatches, no jays or crows. It was as if every living creature was holding its breath.

Aside from a sick, sinking sensation in my stomach, I didn't feel anything. I didn't sense the presence I'd noticed before or feel that creepy pull, that voiceless call that made the hair on my arms tingle. I stopped and shone my flashlight down onto the ground. Mitch's tracks led down the hill. I imagined him making his way down to the pond, using the infrared scope to see his way in the dark, carrying whatever it was he had brought with him to pour or spray into the pond and kill it. Alert, ready for anything.

Then I imagined him walking down that slope in another way, moving against his own will, caught by that thing's spell.

The scream split through the silence like a rocket shell bursting against the black fabric of the receding darkness. It wasn't a person's scream, but it was answered by a yell that had to come from a human throat. As much as that first scream made my knees weak and my heart pound, that answering yell gave me hope. It wasn't a yell of fear, but one of defiance, a warrior's shout.

I started down the hill toward the pond, visible now as a dark pool in the cupped hand of the shadowed valley. Mitch's tracks swung off to the right, but the scream and the answering shout had come from in front of me. I shone the strong beam of my flashlight ahead of me, onto the pond. The last of the thin, late-winter ice was broken, floating in small pieces as if fragmented by something bursting up out of its waters. I trained the beam of the light on the far side of the pond, where the slope was almost vertical and the dead pines with their jagged branches leaned out over the top of the rocky cliff. It was too far away, and all I could see was blurred darkness and the faintest hint of something in shadowy motion. I had to circle around.

I rounded the edge of the pond, close to the base of the cliff. My torch beam picked out something at the base of the cliff. It looked like it had fallen from above, for it was partially buried in the ground. It was a broken spray tank, the kind that firefighters carry in to shoot water onto the hot spots left at the edge of a blaze. I was sure that tank held whatever chemical it was that Mitch had planned to use. I also had a feeling that he hadn't been able to use it.

The tank was only a stone's throw away, but I couldn't get to it without wading—or swimming. The cliff was too close to the water's edge. I shone the light farther, and it showed me something else next to that tank that made my heart sink. Mitch's rifle. The stock of the 30.06 was splintered as if a heavy weight had fallen onto it.

I trained the beam of the light higher. A wide,

long glistening slide of snow stretched from the base up the cliff. Then that slide of snow convulsed and rippled. It moved like a giant slug crawling upward. Its skin was pale, so pale you could see the red and blue pulsing of the organs inside it. It had to be at least fifty feet long, maybe more, and it was twice as thick as a barrel. It wasn't moving fast. It didn't look like the kind of predator that uses speed to catch its prey, though I felt sure that it could strike quickly whenever something came close enough. The way it had grabbed the deer that night. Like a leech, a giant leech, it stretched its body as it crawled slowly upward.

For just a moment I was frozen in shock. A chill ran down my back and my hands trembled. Something was here from our old stories, something that lived to hunt us.

A rock came rolling down from above the creature, bounced off its side without doing any harm, and then landed with a splash in the open water. I shined the light even higher. From the bottom of the cliff to the very top was about two hundred feet. There, just above the creature's head, was Mitch. He was in a climbing harness, trying to pull

himself back up the rope that he'd fastened at the top to let himself down. If he'd been unharmed, it would have been easy for him to do. But the way his left arm dangled told me that he'd been hurt. I couldn't see blood, but it looked as if he was partially paralyzed. He was still climbing, but only a few inches at a time. He had another hundred feet to go. Slow as the progress of the giant leech was, it would get to him before he could reach the top.

Mitch turned his face down toward my light. He didn't say anything, didn't yell again or warn me to get away. I thought, though, that I could make out a grim smile as if he was saying to himself he should have known the dumb kid would butt in. He swung his head up and to the side. Then he went back to trying to drag himself up the rope, which he had looped under his injured arm so that he could steady it.

I got the message. I turned and ran back from the cliff. There had to be a trail Mitch had followed to get to the top. From the lay of the land I was sure I could find it quickly, even without looking for Mitch's tracks in the snow. I was right. There was a rough old deer track snaking its way up through the rocks. I fell once as I scrambled up, and the right knee of my pants tore open. I felt the warm blood from a deep cut flowing down my leg and into my boot, but I paid no attention to it.

By the time I reached the top, the sun was showing itself over the mountain in front of me. The light struck the side of the cliff below me, a sight that I would have appreciated for its beauty another time.

Mitch had driven a pair of pitons into the rock between the roots of the two tallest of the dead pines on top of the cliff. The trees were thinly rooted and the largest one rocked a little as I touched it. I grabbed hold of the line, which thrummed from the tension of the weight on it, and leaned over to look. Mitch was still sixty feet below me.

The great worm was right below him. I could see its head. It was more mouth than head, open and round and gaping, almost like one of those sand worms from *Dune*. Slime was dripping from its round jaws. I remembered what Mitch had told me about how some worms cover their food with slime like that, a caustic juice that starts digesting the food before they even get it into their bodies.

Normally when you are on a climbing line in a harness you can just pull down on the line and it will draw you up, even with one hand. You can do that unless something has a hold of what should be the loose end of the line below you. And that was what was happening now. The great worm had crawled onto, practically glued itself to, the loose end of Mitch's line. He'd now unbuckled himself from the harness and was trying to make his way up the rope using his left leg and his right arm.

It seemed hopeless. I couldn't pull him up because the line was held so tightly below him by the creature. The rope I'd brought was too short to reach him. Even though I didn't like it, I saw what I had to do.

I didn't hesitate. I swung my feet over the edge and let myself down. I'm good at rope climbing. In gym I'm always the first to reach the top. When I reached Mitch I had to crawl over the top of him. I tried to avoid grabbing his bad arm. It didn't look broken, but it seemed paralyzed. His eyes made contact with mine for a brief moment; then he shook his head.

"Shoulda known it," he said in a voice weaker than I expected it to be. "Wannisucka."

I didn't say anything back. It's hard to talk when you have a buck knife held between your teeth. I wrapped one leg around the taut rope and held on with my left hand while I reached down with the knife. The creature's head was no more than ten feet below me and its throat pulsed as it opened its mouth wider.

"Watch out," Mitch yelled from above me. "She's gonna spit at you."

I jerked my head to the side as something came flying out of the mouth of the giant worm. It struck the stones by my face and bounced off. I could see that it was hard and white and shiny and shaped like a two-foot-long lance that was yellow at its tip. I knew now what had paralyzed Mitch's arm. The great worm closed its mouth and seemed to suck in.

Getting ready to shoot off another dart, I thought. Great.

I stuck the knife back between my teeth and fumbled my backpack around to my chest. I reached inside, trying to keep calm.

It'll be okay if I can do this before the count of ten.

Don't ask me why I thought that. You don't always make sense when you're in a tight spot.

One, I counted under my breath, *two* . . . I found what I was looking for in the pack. *Three, four* . . . The worm was starting to open its mouth again. *Five, six* . . . I tore the top off and struck the cap. *Seven, eight* . . . The great worm's mouth was pulsing. *Nine* . . . And then the flare sparked into red fizzing life and I dropped it into the monster's open maw.

I don't know how a worm can scream, whether it has vocal cords or whatever. Maybe, like bumblebees, which absolutely are not supposed to be able to fly according to a study once done by an aeronautical engineer, there's no explanation. But whether it was possible or not, that giant worm screamed. It was so shrill and loud that I thought I would lose my grip and fall. It lifted its head and pounded it against the stones below me so hard that the whole cliff shook and stones broke free.

I had the buck knife out of my teeth now and I was sawing at the rope. The weight at the lower end made it easier to cut through. When it gave way, the great worm started to slide back down the cliffside. I scrambled up hand over hand, crawled over the top of Mitch, and dragged myself to the top of the cliff. Then I grabbed the rope and began to pull.

Mitch helped as much as he could, holding on tight with that one good arm. He was getting some feeling back in the other arm, and that helped. Whatever was in that mammoth worm's darts wasn't deadly; it just immobilized. As I pulled Mitch over the lip of the cliff, I looked back down and I wasn't happy about what I saw. The creature had slid back a ways but it hadn't given up. While I had been pulling, it had started crawling up with new determination.

Mitch tried to stand up, but his feet wouldn't hold him. We didn't have the rifle. I could drop another flare. But then another idea came to me. It was a crazy thought and I had no idea if it would work, but I had to try it. I paused for a moment and closed my eyes. I concentrated all my energy on thinking of wings, dark, flapping wings, filling the sky. My mind filled with that image of hundreds of wings and I started to feel dizzy. Not sure if my plan had worked, I opened my eyes. My gaze fell immediately on the dead pine tree that was leaning over the cliff edge. I began to push on it and Mitch crawled over to add his weight to mine. The tree began to rock back and forth, a little farther each time. The brittle roots creaked and complained in the stone and thin soil, just this side of breaking.

The worm, though, was almost lifting its head over the cliff edge. We might not have made it if not for the crows. They answered my call—it had worked. A whole flock of them came whipping out of the forest and over the top of the cliff. Cawing like crazy, they dove down past us. They circled the great worm, sharp beaks tearing at its back and sides. The air filled with the sound of crow war cries. The great worm stopped trying to climb, and the top quarter of its body reared back, rippling and lengthening. Its head swung back and forth, ducking from its tormenters.

The tall dead pine we'd been pushing, the old tree with dead branches like spikes, broke free and toppled over. I almost went with it, but Mitch grabbed my belt. I leaned over the edge of the cliff and saw the tree strike the monster right in the center of its body. Long, sharp branches stabbed deep into the pale, pulsing skin. The creature convulsed and wrapped its body around the tree, piercing itself again and again with the branches. The weight of the tree slowly forced it back, and then suddenly it tore free from the cliff and fell.

It didn't reach the water. With a loud, echoing crash, the tree wedged itself at the base of the cliff, with the giant worm still impaled and wrapped about it. For a while the creature's body rippled and throbbed. Then the only movement was the flapping of the crows' wings and the bobbing of their heads as they tore pieces of flesh from its body. Other birds were flying in. Hundreds of them, it looked like. This was a feast that could last them for days. Some of them looked up at me and *ca-awked* in what sounded like gratitude—much better than those little boxes of raisins and bags of peanuts.

I looked over at Mitch.

"Hey," he said.

"Hey," I said back. Hollywood movie dialogue it wasn't, but it seemed right at the time.

Then Mitch looked back down to the foot of the cliff. "I don't care if the thing is dead," he said. "I'm still spraying that pond with vermicide."

17

THE LETTER

I T WAS ONE of those rare balmy days that
sometimes come in April to the north country.
The snow had melted away from the southern slope of the hillside where the fox den had

been dug deep into the sandy earth.

I sat there with my shirt open, leaning back on the hillside. Red-and-green lichen mottled the ancient gray-and-black stones on the cliff. Little infusions of quartz sparkled like diamonds. The tangle of blueberry bushes and small spruces that had rooted themselves on its steep sides patterned the cliff with shadow and texture. A pair of blue jays were hopping around in the branches of the cedar tree across from me. They refused to scram—even though I had given them the very last of the peanuts from my pocket. A hopeful-looking crow sat in the top of a nearby little birch tree, *ca-awking* at me as he swayed back and forth.

Darned birds never leave you alone. But it wasn't worth my effort to tell the crow to get lost. Plus I had good reason to be grateful. I found one more box of raisins, spilled them into my palm, and held my hand so the crow could reach those raisins from its perch.

My friend, the mother fox, was sitting next to me. Mouth open, tongue hanging out, she looked with me out over the quiet valley. She seemed to be enjoying the view. Or maybe she was just enjoying a little vacation from the attentions of her four pain-in-the-neck cubs, who were now crawling all over me. The little pests had gotten it into their heads that I was some kind of relative, a large, strangely built uncle, perhaps. One of them had a mouthful of my hair and was growling as he tugged at it. Two others were chewing on my shoelaces. The fourth, who already had a small cross on his back like his mother, was sitting in my lap and staring at my face. I had the uncomfortable premonition that he was planning an assault on my nose. Of the four, he was the worst. Lord knows how his mother could put up with him.

I was keeping such a close watch on those cubs that I hardly heard the sound of the footsteps approaching. When they got too close, just as the top of a person's head began to appear on the trail, the mother fox gave a short yip. Just like that, all four cubs quit their devilment and bolted for the entrance to the den, disappearing in a scuttle of leaf litter and sand—some of which got kicked right into my face. With one last quick look at me, their mother followed behind.

I got the message—not only was I supposed to keep bringing them food, I was deputized to defend them from whomever was coming. They had nothing to worry about. The face that appeared on top of a long lanky frame was that of one of the more harmless humans I know—my friend Devo. I was surprised. I'd told him about the fox den and where it was but I never expected him to be able to find it.

The crow stared at him, took the last raisin, and flapped off.

Devo's mouth was open as he looked at me. "Were those fox cubs?" he said.

"Forget about it," I growled.

Devo grinned at me. "Or what? Or you'll flatten me."

"Exactly."

Devo nodded. "Well, at least I understand why the ladies in the mess hall have been giving you those packets of leftover chicken parts."

I ignored him. The only sensible thing to do.

But he was on a roll and not about to stop.

"Armie, my man, do you know what the other kids call you?"

I squinted my eyes at him. "I don't know," I growled. "Whatever it is, they don't dare say it to my face."

"Take a guess." Devo smiled down at me. It was that darn smile of his that says he knows something you don't know.

I should have flattened him. Instead I took a guess. "Killer?"

Devo shook his head. "Do you really believe that?"

"Mad Dog?"

Devo laughed out loud, sat down next to me, and actually punched me in the arm with his bony knuckles. "Armie," he said, "they call you St. Francis."

"What?" I was outraged.

"Well, what do you expect? Do you see anyone else with birds flapping around their heads and rabbits running up to them to have their heads scratched? Foxes acting like you're their bloody father? It was either that or Dr. Dolittle."

I glowered at him. What about the way people turn their faces away from me as I walk along? Could they be smiling as they did that? They couldn't be. No way. And even though people usually said hi to me, they just did that because they're scared to get on my bad side—right?

"No," I said. "They're all afraid of me."

"Why?"

"Because of my tough attitude, because of the way I look. I scare people."

"Who?"

I stared up at him. "Lots of people. Anytime there's a fight, you know I'm right in the middle of it."

"Breaking it up, you mean," Devo said. "Or stopping some big guy from picking on some little guy."

I started to protest, but Devo held up a long hand.

"Granted," he said, "you are stronger than anybody else at the school. But you don't use that strength to push anyone around. Everybody likes you, Armie—you just don't realize it. They say the school is a way better place since you've been here. But everyone knows how shy you are, so they don't push it with you. They give you space out of respect."

"No way," I said.

"Way," Devo replied. "Name even one person you have beat up."

I had him now. "You," I said. "Remember how I flattened you when we first met?"

He laughed at me. Can you believe that?

"Oh yes," he said, "you flattened me all right. But you didn't mean to do it. You just spun around so fast when I started messing with you that your elbow hit me in the face and knocked me down. But you pulled me up and started falling all over yourself apologizing to me. Face it, Armie, as a bully you are a complete and total failure."

I stared at him with my mouth open. If he wasn't my friend, I would have flattened him.

"You are an idiot," I said.

"Exactly," he replied.

Knowing it was unwise to push his luck any

further, he kept his mouth shut for a while. But only for a while. After all, he was Devo.

"It's too bad," he said, "you never got together with that other Indian, the one on the grounds crew, the one I told you about who was feeding the birds. I noticed yesterday he wasn't around. When I asked the head groundskeeper, he said the man just quit after being on the job only a few weeks. So I presume you'll never get to know him. More's the pity. You two likely would have had a bit in common."

More than you know, I thought. A letter from Mitch was in my coat pocket. It had been addressed to Armin Katchatorian, but the name he called me by in the letter wasn't Armie.

"Quoshtoki," it read, "I'm almost done with my thesis. You and I are the only ones who know just how much I have to leave out of it!"

At the end he said he was planning on taking me up on that offer to come and meet my family in July.

If they are home, I thought.

I hadn't heard from Mom and Dad for two

weeks. I was beginning to feel like an orphan. Maybe they'd decided to stay in Switzerland for good and farm me out to boarding schools for the rest of my life. Or maybe they would be back by the summer and then Mitch could visit us. After all, Mitch wrote, he had family in the area anyhow, including that sixteen-year-old female cousin he was certain I'd like to meet.

Yeah, sure, I thought, if she likes guys who are built like a badger and have the personality of a ground sloth.

But I'd read that part of the letter three times and probably would have gone for a fourth if those blasted fox cubs hadn't gotten so rambunctious that I had to put it away to keep the little good-for-nothings from eating it.

Devo looked back down the hill at the pond. It no longer looked dark. In fact, it glittered with light in the April sun. I'd seen a deer drinking from it early that morning.

"Think that pond would be a good one to swim in?" Devo said.

"Could be." I leaned back and closed my eyes.

Even with Devo bugging me, this was a good place to be.

"So," Devo said, "you planning on spending your whole Saturday here?"

"Maybe," I said.

Devo stood up with one of those smug looks on his face. "Well," he said, "I guess I'll just have to tell your mom and dad that Pits and Hester and me will be the only ones joining them for dinner at the Mirror Lake Inn tonight."

I sat up and grabbed at Devo, but he jumped out of the way.

"What?" I said. "My mom and dad aren't here."

"If it is not them, then it is two very talented impostors who say they just got back from Geneva and drove all the way up here to surprise their son, take him and his friends out to dinner, and then spend the weekend with him."

Devo delivered that message over his shoulder as he ran down the trail. He knew it was wise to do so if he wanted to preserve his worthless life.

"Idiot," I yelled. "You're done for."

Then I went pounding after him. Even though

he thinks he's faster than me because his legs are so much longer, I passed him half a mile farther down the trail.

Quoshtoki. No one can outrun a waterfall.

JOSEPH BRUCHAC is the author of SKELETON MAN, as well as numerous other critically acclaimed novels, poems, and stories, many drawing on his Abenaki heritage. THE DARK POND was inspired by traditional tales still told by the Senecas, Shawnees, and other northeastern American Indian nations about murky waters that hide hungry and terrible creatures. Mr. Bruchac and his wife, Carol, live in upstate New York in the same house where he was raised by his grandparents.

Visit him online at www.josephbruchac.com